More than a year had passed since the unexplained plague had taken all but the little children. Lisa sat alone in her room on the top floor of the fortress-like building. The images of her parents, and by now even her house on Grand Avenue, had become fuzzy. She tried to recall those things more clearly. But it was no use. Lisa returned to her task of writing a constitution.

But out on the rooftop and throughout the halls a celebration was in progress. The new city—an enormous brick high school called Glenbard—could no longer be kept secret.

And watching from dozens of dark places surrounding the school, the other children now understood the strange happenings of the past weeks. They were amazed by what they saw and heard. And the wind carried the nearly forgotten smell of popcorn.

O. T. (Terry) Nelson founded one of the most successful house-painting enterprises in the country, College Craft Enterprises, which has become nationally known as an example of the libertarian philosophy at work. In 1976 he sold his business to travel and to write. Currently living in Minneapolis, Minnesota, Mr. Nelson is working on sequels to this book.

Bla!

—THE——————•
GIRL WHO
OWNED
A CITY

O. T. NELSON

LAUREL-LEAF
BOOKS

For Lisa and Todd

Published by
Bantam Doubleday Dell Books for Young Readers
a division of
Bantam Doubleday Dell Publishing Group, Inc.
1540 Broadway
New York, New York 10036

ISBN: 0-440-92893-1

RL: 5.1

Reprinted by arrangement with Lerner Publications Company

Printed in the United States of America

October 1977

OPM 41 40 39 38 37

Animals, maybe, aren't so lucky.
All they do is what they do—
what their instincts tell them.
They can't invent plans, and make
choices, and dream about tomorrow.

"Good! This house is empty." And while the girl waited in the cold to be sure, she relaxed for a moment and let herself think about the past.

At this very time last Tuesday, she had been sitting, patiently, in fifth-grade social studies. There had been no reason to believe that her life would ever change. But it had, and now it seemed suddenly terrible. The whole world had changed.

"What will happen to me?" she wondered. Then, abruptly, she swung her leg with all her might, and her boot crashed through the glass of the front door.

The shatter-sound was still ringing in her ears as she reached up through the broken pane for the latch. Her movements were quick. She was becoming a good thief.

Her eyes struggled to adjust to the strange dimness of the room. "Lucky—I didn't cut myself that time," she thought, inspecting her hand. But it was trembling, and that made her angry. "There is nothing to be afraid of here! They are gone for good, probably dead. I wonder if I'll ever get used to this."

She promised never to be afraid again, and to prove it, she screamed at the top of her voice, "I'm here, *nobody*, I'm here!"

Not even an echo replied.

The living room was filled with expensive,

comfortable-looking furniture. The big couch seemed especially inviting, and it made the girl realize how tired she was.

Not thinking very clearly, she searched about the room for a light switch. When she finally found one, an ironic little smile formed on her lips. "Dummy!" she thought. "There isn't any electricity anymore."

A bulging lady's purse caught her eye and, without opening it, she threw it into her empty sack.

The odor of spoiled food drew her to the kitchen. The garbage container was crawling with little worms. Someone had told her they were called "maggots," but she didn't like that word—or the fact that they seemed to be in every kitchen. There was something ugly about them. It was almost as if they were tiny ghosts who had moved in to haunt the empty houses.

The refrigerator was filled with warm, rotten food. She started to reach for some apples that still looked good, but she stopped, guessing that they had picked up the taste of the bad food.

In the pantry, she filled her sack almost to the top with canned food—mostly soup. From the bathroom, she added toothpaste, aspirins, Kleenex, and two bars of soap.

"Can opener!" she remembered, and hunted around in the kitchen until she found one. Her bag was filled. Grabbing some candles from the dining room table, she started for the front door.

Her actions lately had become almost automatic. But the girl was still amazed at her ability to do the things she had to do—the things that her ten years of life in a very civilized world just hadn't prepared her for. She had heard the word "looting" before and knew that it was a kind of stealing. They had looted in the California riots. She remembered that from *Current Events*.

But this wasn't really stealing, was it? Whoever owned this house would never be back to claim it. The food and supplies would just go to waste or be claimed by some other children. Besides, the things she took would save her life—and Todd's.

She moved to the light of a window to look at her watch. It was getting close to four o'clock, and Todd would be worried about her. The little guy that she used to find so bothersome now depended on her for everything. He had become the best thing she had.

After tucking the watch into her coat pocket, she started toward the door again but paused, noticing a small writing desk near the window. How neatly the papers were arranged on its top. She couldn't resist the temptation to discover something about the people who had lived in the house. When she sat down at the desk, she felt suddenly very tired. She glanced again at the couch.

"I feel like Goldilocks," she thought playfully. "If only I was." The wish was almost serious. "Then I could have a bowl of warm porridge and take a nap." But there was no time for resting.

Most of the letters on the desk were about business. As nearly as she could figure out, Mr. Williams had been the president of a company that made some kind of tools. There was a stack of partly addressed Christmas cards and one small sealed letter, marked "special delivery—urgent." She opened it.

Master John Williams
Chandler Military Academy
Atlanta, Georgia

Dear Son,
     I have talked seriously with Dr. Chaldon and

he offers no hope to your mother and I. We are both very weak and at the most, we have only a few more days to live. Most of the neighbors are already gone. It's horrible.

On the last news broadcast, November 10th, they said the virus was spreading all over the world. It's the worst plague in history.

They say that for some strange reason the sickness is not fatal to children under the age of about 12 years. The latest reports claim that *no adult* can survive the infection. As crazy as it sounds, soon there may be no adults left in the world, anywhere. I hope that doesn't happen.

But you, Son, are too close to the "unsafe" age to take any chances. Please contact my friend Dr. Coffman in Atlanta at 456 Peachtree Street. He has promised to save you some of the new vaccine that has been working for many young people your age. Don't take *any* chances. Please go to see him the minute you get this letter.

I would have telephoned you, but the Illinois Telephone Company has gone out of business. They say that the postal system can only hold out for another ten days. I hope they'll be able to get this letter through.

I'm sorry that we never got around to that camping trip in Canada. There are many other plans and dreams that will be lost in this incredible tragedy.

Your mother and I would be happy to think that you will take this house when we're gone. And the cottage, of course, is yours too.

We love you, Son. Be brave.

Dad

She put the letter aside, recalling fondly that she had received one very much like it. Her father had sent it from the DuPage County Hospital shortly before he died.

Leaving the front door wide open, she hurried away. John Williams, if he was still alive, wouldn't need a key.

TWO

Her house on Grand Avenue was just four blocks away.
The girl raced down Lenox, toward Oak. That street
was so different now. By her calculations, she had
walked it more than two thousand times, to and from
school, since kindergarten. But now there was no more
school, and almost every house on Oak Street (and every other street, for that matter) looked deserted. No
cars moved. No children played. The houses were dark
and silent. Were there children inside those houses? It
was hard to tell—everyone was hiding. It was eerie.

As she rounded the corner onto Grand, she thought
about how the older children had hated the grown-up
generation. Now they, and what they had called "The
Establishment," were gone. Ten years old in November,
and now *she* was part of "The Establishment." But
there was nothing very established about anything anymore.

Her thoughts were interrupted as she passed the second house on Grand Avenue. Jill Jansen blocked her
path. "What's in the bag?" she asked. "Here, can I take
a look?"

After rustling through the contents, Jill demanded a
few cans of soup for "her" children. Ever since the
Plague, she had been taking homeless children into her
house. She even had a sign in front saying "Children's

House," which Charlie had ripped off the Montessori School for her. The Jansen house was filled with children, and they ate a lot.

"Jill," said the girl, "Todd and I will need all these things. I've been out searching for four days now, and this is the first stuff I've found." But she was unable to resist Jill's arguments, and she gave her four cans of soup, some charcoal, and a book of matches.

Jill hadn't seen the can opener beneath the soup. That was lucky! They were valuable now, and she would have wanted it. Most homes had electric openers which, of course, were useless. "With all those kids around," the girl thought, "why can't they go out and find their own food?"

Todd was waiting at the door. "Lisa, I'm hungry!"

"I know, Todd, but look what I found for us. Soup and matches. I was afraid we would run out. Hide the food in the space under the stairs. Give me the matches. I'll light the charcoal."

Dinner was simple—it had to be—soda crackers and soup heated over the barbecue grill. They had powdered milk, made with water from Lake Ellyn that Lisa boiled to make safe.

They ate in silence, and Lisa thought about their strange new life. There were no more conveniences like cooking gas or running water. No fresh milk and eggs. No fruit, bread, butter, or ice cream. All the things that they had once taken for granted were gone. But at least there was their home, and the empty houses where she could search for supplies. But that source couldn't last long. The grocery stores had been looted already, and even they were empty of anything worthwhile.

She was thinking now, of last Tuesday, or was it Wednesday? She couldn't remember. She and Todd had pulled a wagon to the White Hen Pantry at Five Corners, hoping to find supplies, but someone had thought of the idea first. The glass door was smashed and the shelves were empty of all the things that children liked. The cash register had been broken open. "What will those kids do with the money?" she wondered. "Money is useless now. There are no places to spend it."

She'd never forget the happy look on Todd's face when he found a kite that had fallen behind the candy counter. "Todd, you dummy. We won't have time to play with kites," she had said, and then she instantly promised herself that they would find the time. "Oh, all right. Put it in the wagon."

Lisa used to hate her brother sometimes, for getting more attention than she got. But now she didn't. He was a good boy. She needed him very much and treated him as though she was his mother. It was strange how even this had changed. Everything was all upside down.

The shelves of the store were not completely empty though. They were well stocked with all of the things that children don't like. There were cans of asparagus and spinach. She took them. The vitamin and medicine rack was still full. She emptied it. Lisa couldn't understand why the first invaders had left things like candles, paper plates, and instant breakfast. She took those things also. Soon the small wagon was filled. Todd pushed an empty grocery cart toward her and they began filling it with other supplies. Lisa laughed, thinking of the stomachaches those first invaders must have had from all the candy and pop.

In a way, she was glad that those things were all gone. Not that she wouldn't have given anything for some sunflower seeds and a Cherry-Ola Cola, but she knew that Todd wouldn't eat right if the house was filled with treats.

Someone had broken a bag of popcorn, and one aisle

of the store was covered with the unpopped kernels.
Lisa, feeling that this might be the only treat left in the
world for them, scooped several handfuls into her rain-
coat pocket. As they left, the two children looked back
at the White Hen Pantry. It *did* look odd, and she could
remember it now. All the racks and shelves were empty,
except for those with cigarettes and the newspapers
from Thursday, November 20 . . . .

"Can I have some more soup?" Todd's voice interrupted her thoughts.

"Sure. Here, Todd." She gave him what was left in
her bowl, and slipped back into her reverie . . . .

"Is this Sunday?" Lisa wondered, not being sure.
Keeping track of the time was still important. She and
Todd had to plan their days. She had given him Father's watch. When she promised to be back at a certain
time, she would make sure to do so. He wouldn't worry
if he could measure the time by his watch.

Since the Plague, Todd had learned many other new
things. It was one of his daily jobs to dump the garbage
in the Triangle woods across the street. He carried pails
of water from Lake Ellyn and stored it in the downstairs tub. Because Lisa worried about his safety, she
made him carry an empty gun—not that he could actually use it. But she had taught him how to scare people with it.

Though he hated to wash dishes, he *did* volunteer for
that chore and he managed to get them pretty clean.
She thought it was cute to see him perched on the tall
wooden stool by the sink. The dishes were going fast—
he broke at least one each day. Paper plates had been
nice, while they lasted . . . .

"Hurry and get the dishes done, Todd. It's getting
dark." Lisa went outside to put out the charcoal, but

since the coals were still hot, she decided to make some popcorn. The sound and the smell were fun.

There were other children, close by, who remembered the word "fun" when they smelled her corn popping. A pair of eyes appeared in the Harris window, and pretty soon the backyard was filled with popcorn appetites. Those old playmates had spent very little time together since the Plague.

The popcorn was a little burnt and chewy, but it seemed delicious.

The children ate in silence, washing away the salty taste with glasses of Kool-Aid. They were remembering what popcorn parties used to be like.

"Todd, bring the hammer and nails. We've got to board up the living room windows before we go to bed." Todd did as he was told, though he didn't understand why it was necessary.

The gangs had begun to roam at night. For extra protection, Lisa nailed several boards over each window, bending most of the nails before they went into the wood. The job took almost an hour and, by that time, it was dark. The nails were really too small, and any strong man could have ripped the boards away. But they were safe tonight, because no strong man would try to break in. There were no men.

By the light of a Christmas candle, they locked the doors and went to the small room in the basement. The room had no windows and it was, they thought a safe place to spend their nights. In the old days, it had been used by their father as a study. They had never understood why he liked it there—it was so cold and cheerless. But now, after a week of nights in that room, the two children had grown to like it. It felt safe.

They climbed into the small bed to keep each other warm. Lisa was glad to have the little boy with her, and even though he could not express the sentiment, he was glad to have her, too.

"Lisa, please tell me a story," he said. He liked her stories.

For some reason, tears started to form in her eyes and she wanted to cry. It wasn't that she was afraid, really. She was much more confident in herself now and in their ability to survive. She really didn't know why she felt like crying. Since that first day when they were truly alone, Lisa had been too busy for tears. And she had learned that crying did no good.

"Please tell me a story. About . . . about . . . about . . ." He laughed because he still thought his pretended stammer was funny. She laughed too, not because she thought it was funny, but because she wanted to laugh. He was so cute when he tried to be funny. Mom and Dad would have laughed too.

". . . about . . . about Todd and Barney and when they went fishing," he finished.

"Well," she began her familiar story:

Todd and Barney Beagle wanted to help Lisa find food to eat. She was always bringing canned soup and nothing was ever fresh. There was never even any hamburger. So Todd decided he would take the fishing pole out of the garage and get some worms and try to catch fish at Perry's Pond.

It was a warm, sunny day and Todd asked Lisa to take him to the pond. He was afraid of getting lost. She walked with him and made him promise to come home in one hour. Toddy-boy looked at his watch and asked, "Will that be ten o'clock?" She said, "yes." And went back to the house.

Todd put his hook into the water just like Uncle Pete had showed him. Barney was wagging his tail. He liked the sun on his coat.

Nothing happened. No fish would bite. Toddy-boy wondered if there *were* any fish in that dumb pond. Maybe they got sick and died too, he thought.

Then he remembered that he didn't have a worm on the hook, so he pulled out his line and laid it down on the bank and thought a while.

Uncle Pete used to find worms under the leaves in the wet dirt and Todd remembered this. He walked toward a bunch of trees and dug with his hands till he found a small worm. Barney got excited and barked at the worm.

Todd laughed at the image, and Lisa continued.

He went back to the place where his fishing pole was and put the worm on the hook. It looked funny hanging there, but that's the way Uncle Pete did it. He put the line in the water and waited.

He waited and waited, but nothing happened. He said to Barney, "We're not going to quit. We've got to catch a fish. I hate soup."

They waited for a long time and then Todd decided to move to another spot. "Maybe the fish live over by that big rock," he thought, and he dropped his line in the water near the rock. He waited some more. It seemed like forever. He waited and waited. It was almost ten o'clock. "I've just got to catch a fish," he thought. And suddenly, something pulled on his line. Todd pulled back. Barney stood up and barked at the strange flopping in the pond. Out came a fish. It landed on the

grass and flopped all around. Barney went crazy
barking at it.

Todd ran all the way home. He was proud.

Lisa cooked the fish for supper and it was delicious. Much better than soup.

"Did you like that story, Todd?"

"Please tell another one, Lisa," he asked, in a way
that answered her question.

She said, "Tomorrow night, I've got a special story
about Todd and Barney, about how they solved a real
mystery. But now, we must go to sleep."

The little boy did fall asleep, almost instantly. Lisa
tried to sleep, but her mind was too busy thinking about
tomorrow. Maybe Todd would catch a fish, but there
were some other things to be done that were very important.

As Todd fell more deeply asleep, Lisa was alone
once again. During the daytime, she was too busy to
think or feel any loneliness. But at night, in the cold
basement darkness, she could feel it, and she thought
about their odd new life.

During the first nights, Lisa had been fearful and
confused. "What will become of us?" was the question
that seemed to pound at her in the stillness. But grad-
ually, she began to believe that somehow she would find
a way to keep them alive.

They needed food, first of all, but the supply would
soon be gone. The average house contained only
enough for about two weeks. By "dieting," as Lisa liked
to call it, that supply might be stretched to four weeks,
though the four weeks would go by all too quickly.

The stealing helped, but by this time, all the vacant
houses and stores were completely empty. The existing
supplies were going fast.

Could she hunt for food? Lisa laughed at the thought of tramping through the forest preserve with a shotgun. It would never work. Besides, she doubted that she'd have the courage to skin a rabbit even if she was lucky enough to find and kill one.

Fishing was a good possibility. It would be easier than hunting, but there would still be the problem of cutting the poor things up. She could do it, though, she decided. After all, she'd seen her father do it often enough. She would teach Todd how to fish and he could spend some time each day at Perry's Pond. But for the moment, they couldn't depend on any one plan. She must figure out other possibilities.

Could she raise food? Not until spring, and then only if she spent some time during the winter reading about gardening. There was a book about it in the den that she could study.

The thought of gardening gave Lisa a brilliant idea. Tomorrow, she would ride her bike north on Swift Road to some farms she remembered. There, she might find large quantities of food. "Wow! Maybe I can find a live chicken and we can have fresh eggs."

Now she was really getting somewhere.

Her thoughts were interrupted by a sound—a scratching sound in the wall. "It must be a mouse," Lisa decided, after hearing it a second and third time. "I wonder how he survives?"

Animals, she thought, were lucky in a way. They had their instincts to help them survive. It was sort of automatic, the way they knew how to find food in their surroundings. But for people, it wasn't that simple. "We have to invent traps and guns and learn how to raise food. People have to *think* to keep alive."

Lisa had never needed to consider it before. It seemed that food and clothing and television and lights were just there to be used. Now everything had changed. Everything had come to a stop. She saw the answer clearly.

It was *thinking* that gave people all the wonderful things and that kept them alive. But now the grown-ups were gone. She had to face that reality every day. "It will be my thinking that will let us keep on living. I hope my ideas work!"

Todd began to cry in his sleep. Lisa stroked his hair and whispered something soothing. Soon he was quiet again.

It was obvious to the girl that finding food would be a constant and frustrating problem. But at least now she had some good ideas. Her mind seemed clearer. She could—yes, she would—figure something out.

Lisa glanced at the wind-up clock. It was almost ten. "I'd better get to sleep," she decided. But by now her thoughts were racing. Many new ideas were coming to her. Some of them made her laugh, but some were actually workable. It seemed that she had a million things to do tomorrow, and for the first time in weeks, she actually couldn't wait to get started.

It was midnight when she next noticed the face of the clock. Lisa smiled in the dark. For the first time in her quiet, bedtime aloneness, she felt happy and confident. Animals, she thought, maybe weren't so lucky. All they do is what they *do*—what their instincts tell them. They can't invent plans, and make choices, and dream about tomorrow.

——— THREE ———————————————————

Monday used to be Girl Scout day.

The old scout uniform caught Lisa's eye, as she scanned her closet for something to wear. It was useless now, she realized. Troop 719 didn't exist. The uniform still belonged to her, but she herself belonged to very little. Once she had been a Girl Scout, a fifth grader, a daughter, a ballet dancer, a friend, and so many other kinds of "belonging" that she couldn't name them all. Now, she belonged only to herself and Todd.

She put on the green dress, and it made her feel good somehow.

The morning chores went faster than usual because she was anxious to start on her trip to the farm. She made the bed, unlocked the house, wound the clocks, dressed, and made the breakfast in less than eighteen minutes.

Todd asked his regular breakfast question, "What will we do today, Lisa?"

She started to tell him that he must try fishing, but hesitated, thinking that she had been too bossy lately. Small as he was, Todd was a real partner and Lisa knew that it would be better if they acted as a team.

"Do you think that you could catch some fish at Perry's Pond?" she asked.

"Sure, Lisa." He was confident.

"Good. I'll help you get the stuff together." Lisa knew her suggestion was better than an order.

"I'll find some worms," Todd volunteered, putting on his coat. "Where's that shovel?"

She helped him find it. As he headed for the Triangle, dragging the huge shovel behind him, she smiled, feeling certain that she would end up digging the worms.

Todd returned from the woods a few minutes later. "He's given up already," thought Lisa. But she was wrong. His face wore a giant smile and his coat pocket was filled with worms, twigs, and leaves. They sorted them out, putting the biggest worms in a coffee can. She strung the bamboo pole and Todd started toward the pond.

"Come back by ten o'clock and don't fall in the water." Then, she thought, "Oops, I'm giving orders again."

"Okay, Lisa."

Then she eagerly began to prepare for her own adventure. On Chidester Street she found a high-sided, red wagon. In it were a few small cars and a toy truck which she decided to bring home for Todd. The wagon itself would be a perfect vehicle for carrying whatever she might find at the farms. At home, she tied the wagon securely to the back of her bicycle. If she did find a chicken, she would need a cage of some kind. The wicker clothes hamper best suited that purpose.

Since she planned to be gone for several hours, she slipped the last candy bar into her coat pocket. It would provide energy until supper. She prepared Todd's snack—soda crackers and a packet of instant breakfast mixed with water. They had a huge supply of this powdered food, and though she hated the taste, she was very glad to have it.

Todd returned at ten o'clock without any fish. His disappointment was hidden behind talk about tomorrow's fishing trip, about how he wanted more time, about how he was sure he could catch fish for them. "Fishing takes patience," he said, in a tone of voice that reminded her of Uncle Pete.

"Tomorrow you'll catch some, Todd," said Lisa, and she thought about what a good boy he really was.

But the patient boy turned back into a sassy little brother when he learned that Lisa was going on a trip without him. He threw a small tantrum. "Why not?" he asked, finally, when he realized that no argument would change her mind.

"Because of the gangs. I've heard them at night. The vacant houses are empty and they are starting to steal from other child-families like us. Soon they will be out in the daytime and we must be careful. I thought you wanted to be the guard of our house?"

"I do, Lisa," he answered. "How long will you be gone?"

"I should be back by three at the latest. Did you wind your watch?"

"Yes."

"Remember," she said, mounting her bike, "stay in the house, keep the doors locked, and if anyone should try to break in, hide quiet as a mouse in the crawl space under the stairs. Keep the gun with you all the time. Your chocolate milk is on the table."

As she rode off, the wagon clattered along behind her, making more noise than she would have liked. Once on Riford Street, she looked back and saw a few small faces peek from the door of a boarded-up house. She pedaled as slowly as possible, but the metal wagon still banged loudly.

A girl from Beth Bush's house recognized her and

began to run to meet her, but for some reason, she stopped abruptly after two or three paces and ran back inside. Lisa saw this from the corner of her eye and wondered what had stopped the girl.

"Who of my friends would be living at the Bush's house?" she wondered. It looked vaguely like Becky Cliff, but her appearance made it hard to be sure. Whoever it was had not been too lucky. Her face was pale and smudged with dirt. Her hair and clothes looked quite neglected.

"Those kids are probably wondering what I'm up to. They can see that I'm off to find supplies, but I bet they can't guess why I'm headed *away* from houses and stores. I hope I'm the first to think of the farm idea. I'll be mad if I pedal all the way out there just to find them empty like everything else."

Lisa's leg muscles began to ache even before she reached North Avenue, but her mind was so occupied with thoughts of the farm that she didn't notice the pain. "There just has to be lots of food there," she thought. "After all, that's where food is raised."

At North Avenue, she decided to rest her legs. And so, pulling the bike into the deserted Arco station, she sat for a while in the sun, using a gas pump for a backrest. The candy bar made her thirsty. She found a water faucet and walked toward it, hoping that enough pressure remained in the tank to force out a little trickle of water. To her surprise, the water came rushing out. The long drink refreshed her, and she returned to her seat by the pump.

As she sat, staring at the big highway, Lisa became aware of its stillness. Not one single car. Not a sign of life anywhere. It was so silent.

All her other visits to this intersection had been in

the family car. They had waited patiently every time for a break in the stream of cars. But now there was no traffic at all and the road seemed huge and odd without it.

Somewhat playfully, she thought, "Now's my chance to break a rule without getting punished." The rule was that you should always look both ways before crossing a street.

She gained momentum on her bike, held her eyes straight ahead, and crossed the intersection without looking to either side. She laughed out loud, and then said, "Many rules have become useless." But that remark was without humor.

In fifteen minutes, Lisa reached the farms. She chose the one that looked most inviting. It had a long white fence that disappeared into trees on either side and many large, freshly painted buildings. She parked her bike by the largest building.

What she saw inside the main barn made her feel sick. The cows had been closed in their stalls with too small a supply of food. They had all been dead for some time. It was a horrible sight and she stood for only a moment in the midst of it.

Afraid to venture into the other farm buildings, she turned her attention to the field crops. There were none. The farmer had already harvested whatever he raised and nothing remained in the fields but clods of dirt and brown stubs.

Lisa looked toward the farmhouse. Strangely, the rear door was wide open. Inside, it was clear to Lisa that the house had never been looted. Aside from evidence that a few small squirrels had moved in, the rooms had not been entered since the death of the owners.

A note lay on the kitchen table.

To the finder of this note:

We have loved this farm and our family has worked it for over forty years. Now we must give it up and we have no children to leave it to.

Please come to live on our farm. The cattle will give you fine milk. The chickens can give you eggs. If you look in my husband's study, you will find a case of books and notes that will help you learn all you need to know about farming.

In a world without adults, you will need a simple way to live. Take this farm. It makes us happy to think that some young children will choose our place to make their new lives.

Sincerely,
Winifred Crowl

P.S. The cookie jar is filled with oatmeal and chocolate chip cookies. The pantry has a good supply of canned goods.

On the back side were scribbled these final words. The handwriting was very poor.

I think I am the last to die. I know of no other adult who is still alive. I tried to get out to feed the cattle or let them go, but I fainted and had to come back inside.

I've waited and waited. I thought you might even come around while I still breathed, but now I don't think so.

While I wait, I think about you and what fear your new life must give you—to be alone in a world without the grown-ups that once made it run. There must be fear and sadness all around you. Be brave, children, be strong.

You must figure out how to make things work
again—like this farm and the other things that
make life so easy. You can do it. It will take time
and work, but you can do it . . . .

Another sentence was started and then crossed out.
Maybe the woman didn't have the time to finish it. Or
more likely, she just couldn't dream up any good advice
for the new world. She couldn't begin to imagine what
that world would be like. "And I can see why," thought
Lisa.

But she had come pretty close. And with her first
real tears in a long while, Lisa surrendered to the kindness in the woman's words. "All this time I've been
truly alone and her note . . . it's . . . it's like the last
words I'll ever hear from those people."

She sat in silence for a long time, letting the woman's
words repeat themselves in her mind. "Be brave . . .
strong . . . find out how it runs . . . ." Lisa knew that
they would not take over the farm—they loved their
own home too much.

Then she forced herself to think of the present emergency. "No time to waste here." She shook herself back
into action. As she went out the back door, she carried
a large bag filled with flour, canned vegetables, and
other supplies from the pantry. A chicken darted
around the corner of the house and hurried toward her
with a haste that seemed to say, "I'm glad to see you."
Lisa was definitely glad to see the hen, and with no effort at all, she put the bird into the wicker basket.

She was swept up in a sudden mood of happiness.
Although she didn't find all that she had hoped for,
Lisa took with her some encouragement from a sweet
woman, homemade cookies, and a live hen. If only her
wagon wasn't so small . . . .

And in this joyous mood, a reckless idea came to her. An idea that made her laugh a bold, confident laugh. "Instead of making endless supply trips with the bike and wagon, I will learn to drive the car. Today!"

Of course she could do it! "Put the gas pedal all the way to the floor, pump it three times, leave it halfway down, and turn the key." Her father's words ran through her mind. He had said them so many times to her mother, sometimes apologizing for his bossiness. But now she was happy that she remembered his repetitious directions. They would give her enough to go on. She would soon remember the others and she would be driving! Lisa couldn't wait to see the bewildered look on the faces of the Riford Street kids when she made her first trip—actually driving a car.

She barely noticed the passing scene on her bike ride home. She was thinking about the car ride. She could do it! As she passed North Avenue, the gas station, and the blank, peering faces on Riford Street, she was rehearsing the details of her adventure. Her father's instructions came to her clearly now, as if they had been stored on tape somewhere in her brain, waiting to be called into use. "Keep it in park till you're ready to go . . . let it warm up a few minutes . . . look all around you . . . keep your foot on the brake . . . put the shift lever in drive . . . let up on the brake . . . not too much gas. . . slowly now . . . ."

The driveway of her house appeared. Quickly, she pulled the wagon and bike into the garage. The sight of the big car made her stomach feel funny. "I'll never . . ." she started to speak, but stopped, knowing that she *must* try it. She emptied the wagon, and called Todd to tell him her plans.

"Really?" Todd was excited. "Let's go now!"

"I didn't say *we*, Todd. I must go alone." It was too

late to avoid his outburst. She wished that she had told
him another way. But finally he stopped arguing, and
she made peace with him. "It's dangerous and I must
learn how to drive first. You can go some other time."

Lisa drew a map of her course, and he understood it
when she traced the route to North Avenue with her
finger. "If I'm not back by three-thirty, come looking
for me."

He watched her climb into the car. "Be careful,
Lisa." His warning surprised her. She wondered if he
was imagining his own fate if something actually did go
wrong.

Behind the wheel, she struggled to adjust the seat.
Even on the thick cushion she seemed swallowed up by
the dashboard. Her feet just barely touched the pedals.
Lisa was frightened. Ten-year-old girls just *didn't* drive
cars. What made her think that *she* could?

Her body shook in silence for a long time. "Damn
tears!" And then she laughed at her first real swear
word. Somehow it made her feel better, and, wiping the
blur from her eyes, she said it again. "We need those
supplies and it would take ten trips with the wagon. Besides, someone else might find the stuff before I can get
it all moved. If I can learn to drive this thing, then we
can really stock up. That will give me time to make better plans."

The future had not been very clear to her before this,
but now she could imagine months and years of finding
food and trying to survive. The car would help a lot.
"Good," she thought, looking at the fuel gauge, "it's full
of gas. I'm glad the car is facing out to the street. I'd
never be able to back it out."

She remembered the instructions again. "Put the gas
pedal all the way to the floor, pump it three times, leave
it halfway down, and turn the key." The engine came

alive with a powerful roar, and as if frightened by the sound, her foot jumped from the pedal and the roar became a soft whir.

"Look all around you." As Lisa recalled the command, her eyes traced a circle around the car . . . and they passed a pale boy framed by the side of the garage door.

"Keep your foot on the brake . . . put the shift lever in drive . . . let up on the brake . . ." and the car crept forward.

"Here I go." The words were trapped in her throat. "Slowly," she reminded herself.

It seemed to Lisa that she was flying to the end of the driveway. She turned the wheel a little too sharply, and drove across the Cole's grass. The crunching sound was the end of Larry's motorcycle. He would have been angry.

"Not too much gas . . . slowly . . . ." Her foot hadn't touched the gas pedal and yet she was still moving. "Why am I moving? Is something wrong?" In panic, she stepped hard on the brake. The car screeched to a violent stop, bringing her head against the steering wheel with a painful crash. It was too late to recall her father's words, "easy on the brakes." Lisa was stunned. The car stopped; the engine was silent.

In a few moments her head was clear again, but it ached above the right eye. "Dummy," she thought. "Easy on the brakes!" She wouldn't make that mistake again.

The nervousness began to leave her. She started the engine again and set off very slowly this time, completely unaware of the many astonished eyes that followed her.

Her whole body was working to control the motion of the car. She felt as though she had become a part of the machine—the most important part. "Don't you worry, Toddy-boy. I'll be back soon."

For weeks, Lisa had longed for the sight of a moving automobile. It would have meant that not all the adults were gone—that the nightmare wasn't true. Now she was thankful that there was no traffic. It made her present task much easier.

Slowly, safely, she guided the car toward the farm. Down Riford, to St. Charles, to Swift Road, across North Avenue. On the straight stretches of road, she practiced controlling the brake and gas pedals. Her top speed of five miles per hour seemed like a hundred.

At the farm, she quickly loaded the car to the ceiling, left, and cautiously inched her way toward home. When the car finally stopped in the driveway, Lisa was deep in thought. "What I've accomplished in one hour would have taken at least six full days with the wagon. If I don't waste gas, this car can save our lives. I never thought about a car in that way before."

Proudly, she honked the horn. Todd ran out to meet her. Together they unloaded the supplies. When the car was empty, she said, "Todd, it's only three o'clock and I have time for another trip. Carry all this stuff into the house. Put all the canned things into the hiding place under the stairs. Put the flour and fresh vegetables into the freezer . . . . Yes, I know the freezer doesn't work, but it will be a good storage space that we can lock. If there isn't enough room, you can fill the washer and dryer."

"Why the washer and dryer?" Todd wondered.

"So the gangs can't find it if they break in. You can put all the tools and other stuff that isn't food in the furnace. Just slide up the furnace door."

He stared at the huge pile of food. "Okay, Lisa, but hurry back. I'm hungry."

"Here, Todd," she pulled some cookies from her pocket. "I've got a surprise treat for tonight. You'll like it." The cookies were gone before she got the car started again.

As she drove away, some new hidden eyes followed her. But this time their expression was not astonishment. It was something quite different altogether.

"I should have been more careful," thought Lisa. "Maybe a gang saw the load I brought home. It was dumb to honk the horn and leave that stuff in the driveway, with Todd unprotected."

Lisa hurried back from the farm and found the driveway empty. She thought, "That little rascal, he must have run up the stairs with every load. I'll give him two stories tonight," she promised, happily.

Realizing all that had to be done before dark, Lisa rushed to unload the supplies in the garage. They could hide them later if necessary. She was tired, and rested a moment against the car before making another trip to the garage. "What a magnificent thing, that car . . . ."

A rock smashed the rear windshield. A laughing voice dissolved into the Triangle woods. In an instant, it all became clear. "Todd, Todd," she cried as she ran into the house. Where was he? She searched the rooms. He was gone. "Todd, Todd." No answer.

Walking near the hiding place, she knew where he was. The light from the opened door fell upon his sobbing figure. He was bleeding.

"Oh, Todd . . . oh, Todd." He looked at her and clung to her. Nothing more was said while she soothed him.

Finally she asked, "What happened?"

"I . . . I . . . was bringing things into the house when they came. They took our food, Lisa. They were mean to me, Lisa."

"Don't worry, Todd. It will never happen again. Who were they?"

"I don't know. They pushed me and hit me and said we couldn't have that stuff." He stopped crying.

She studied his injuries and found them to be nothing more than a bloody lip and some minor bruises. She dried his tears, and with a towel, blotted the blood from his lip. "Rest here on the couch and I'll make a special supper."

He was pleased when she served the Spam and noodles, and the fright of his experience disappeared altogether with the candy bar dessert.

The gang had only taken what was in the driveway. Unfortunately, that had included the chicken. But they hadn't bothered to look in the house. Perhaps her early return interrupted their plans, though she couldn't imagine why they would be afraid of *her*.

Before securing the house that evening, Lisa locked the car and hid the key.

Later in their small, dark room, she stared into the candle. She was too tired to blow it out and her mind was too excited to permit sleep. She was happy about the day's adventures—all except for the cruelty to Todd. Otherwise, things were beginning to take shape.

"First thing tomorrow, I must find new hiding places for our supplies. We also need some defense. I wonder . . . ." Her thoughts drifted back to their bed and she became aware, without looking, that Todd was wide awake, and thinking too.

"Hey, Todd." Her words sounded loud in the silence of the chamber. "What are you thinking about?"

He avoided her question with one of his own. "Will you tell me a story?"

"Yes, Todd." Lisa thought for a long time and then began.

There was a boy about your age, Todd, who lived many years ago. He and his older sister were living in a poor old house, alone, because their parents were gone, just like ours. The other people of the town were very poor and they didn't have much time to help the two orphans out, so the boy and girl had to take care of themselves.

The town wasn't always poor. There used to be a big factory where most of the men and some of the women worked. But the owner of the factory died and no one wanted to keep it going anymore. Many of the people moved away, but a few families stayed and they got poorer and poorer. Still they stayed.

The father of the boy and girl had a good job in the factory. It was his work to design the candles that were made there. For many years, candles of his design were sold all over the world—some plain, others in beautiful shapes and colors. Christmas was the best time of year for the factory town because they sold thousands of Christmas candles.

The father died suddenly, and their mother kept them alive by raising chickens and vegetables. But one day, she became sick. Her illness lasted a long time and since she had to stay in bed, she taught the boy and girl how to care for the chickens and tend the garden. Each morning they would take eggs and vegetables to the highway and sell them. Their store was a large table with a sign that the girl had made. When their mother died, the children kept on with the chickens and the vegetables and the stand on the highway. They earned very little, but it was enough to buy food. There was no school. In fact, their life was sort of like ours is now.

One day while the girl was at the highway selling eggs and vegetables, some boys came to steal the chickens. They were mean to the little boy and hit him. He was afraid, and sad too, because he couldn't stop them. He knew that the chickens were very important to them.

When the girl came home and found what had happened, she cried a lot. The little boy cried too, because he knew that if his sister cried, it must be very bad. She hardly ever cried.

The little boy went to bed and thought about what would become of them. He thought he was no good to anyone and he said to himself over and over again, "You couldn't fight those boys or even save the chickens." He thought, sadly, that there wasn't time for him to grow up to be helpful because they would starve first. To himself, he seemed a useless coward.

But suddenly he had an idea that stopped his sad thoughts. He knew that feeling sorry for himself was a waste of time and he knew what had to be done and that he *could* help.

He woke his sister and told her his plan. "When the candle factory was still working, everything was okay. But after the factory stopped, everyone became poor, like us. Let's open the candle factory," he said proudly.

His sister didn't say a word and he thought that she didn't like his idea, but he continued. "We can make candles just like we used to do for Christmas presents. It's easy, and people like candles!" He was excited.

And still, his sister said nothing. He was sure his idea would work and all his cowardly, little-boy thoughts seemed gone forever. "It will work! Don't you think it will work?" he asked.

"Yes," said his sister, "I think you're right, Christmas is coming and people will buy candles. The factory is still sitting there. Maybe we can talk to some of the townspeople to see if they'd want to open the factory again."

The little boy went to sleep, feeling very happy and proud.

The next day, the two children went to see every family in the little town. Nobody wanted to help. They all said, "We don't know how to run a candle factory." Some said they were too busy. Some laughed at the little boy, making jokes about him as a big little businessman.

He didn't care. He was sure his idea would work. He and his sister went to the candle factory to look around. They found that all the candle-making machines had been taken away. All that remained was a supply of wax. But it would be enough to start with. They used what was left of their money to buy more wax and coloring.

They made their candles by hand, heating the wax over the stove and mixing in the color. Before the wax cooled, they poured it into different sizes of cans with string down the middle for the wicks. As the days went by, their candles got better and better. They were too busy to wonder if they would succeed.

The girl made a huge sign saying "Christmas Candles—Fifty Cents," and on Saturday, they both went to the highway. It was one week before Christmas.

Many people stopped to buy candles, telling

them that they were beautiful. By noon of that day, they had sold all their candles, and they had earned thirty-five dollars. They were so happy and excited that they ran all the way back to the factory to make more. By Christmas Eve, they had made over two hundred dollars and they were the happiest children in the world.

At home that night, the girl said, "I have a surprise. Wait in the other room till I call for you."

It seemed like forever, but the boy waited patiently. Finally she called him into the room.

There on the table were three packages, wrapped in Christmas paper. "Merry Christmas!" she said.

He opened them excitedly and found a book, a shiny toy car, and a box of his favorite candy. These were his first presents in three years, and he kissed his sister saying, "But I don't have a present for you. I'm sorry."

"You gave me a wonderful present," she replied. "Your idea has saved us." And they began to talk about their small business and to make plans to really start up the factory again and go to school and many other things.

They talked a long time before the girl blew out their candle. It was the first one that they had made.

"Did you like that story, Todd?"

He said that he wanted another. Lisa told him a short, cheery story about how Todd and Barney found a buried treasure in the Triangle. His mood was changed. Lisa felt that her story had put aside his feelings of self-doubt.

His small body was warm and motionless—except

for the rhythm of his soft breathing. His presence in the still nights had become a real comfort to her.

Everything was still. Lisa liked this quiet time because their problems, and her solutions, seemed so easy in the darkness.

What had to be done was clearer to her now. They needed to hide their supplies—in the walls, in the furniture, under the flooring, in the furnace, and in places that would protect them from any invader. Next, she had to figure out a means of defense. And that, she knew, wouldn't be easy. Perhaps booby traps in the yard would be a good idea, or even better, a fine thread around the house to trigger an alarm that would start an avalanche of rocks falling from the roof. "That's it!" she thought. "Above the front and rear doors . . . and then some new weapons . . . the gun wasn't enough."

When the house was better protected, she could make more trips to the farm. But she had a feeling that the farm's supply wouldn't be nearly enough. Soon the other children would think of the farm idea. Then what would she do? Where would she go for food? She thought and thought and her thoughts turned to dreams . . . dreams about a fantastic place with rows and rows of her favorite foods, stacked to the ceiling.

Sometime in the night, she awoke, thinking of the word "warehouse . . . warehouse . . . a place where groceries are stored." How had the idea come to her? She lit the candle, climbed out of bed and began thumbing, endlessly it seemed, through the large telephone book. Finally, she found what she wanted under "Groceries—Wholesale." "Here it is, a Jewel Grocery Warehouse on North Avenue. Close enough," she thought. "And I'll bet no one else has even thought of it!" Her mind wandered through the fabulous place for a long time, conjuring scenes of the endless supply of food she might find. She must go there soon.

But she couldn't leave Todd alone again—at least until a better defense plan was arranged. She decided to call a meeting of her friends on Grand Avenue to form some kind of militia. By cooperating, they could protect each other from the gangs. If they planned together, they could figure out a way to live, even after the present supplies were gone.

Her thoughts went on and on until they became dreams again. Her parents wouldn't have believed it. They had known that Lisa was smart, but would they have believed that she could survive so cleverly? That she could drive a car or provide for a family?

But Lisa wasn't really ten years old anymore. Everything had changed. The same mind that used to get "A's" in math and English was now struggling to pass a frightening course in survival. True, the old civilization had disappeared, but it had left many clues. It was logical that she should succeed.

──── FOUR ────

Todd awoke, crying, just before dawn. "Probably a bad dream," Lisa thought, "and no wonder, considering all that's happened."

By the time he was asleep again, Lisa was wide awake. She felt that it must be light outside and her clock confirmed it. It was seven. Quietly, she dressed and slipped from the basement room.

Outside, the morning sun warmed her as she studied their house on the hill. It would be easy, she decided, to defend it. But why was such a thing as defense necessary? Of course, she knew why—the children were hungry and frightened. And it wasn't surprising to her that some of them had started stealing from other children. But she just couldn't believe that it was necessary. Couldn't they find a better way? Still, there was no time to waste in preparing the defense. Her mind worked quickly to plan the day's labors.

Lisa's attention turned to the car. It had been a brilliant idea, and she didn't mind giving herself a compliment. Yes, brilliant—almost like inventing something, even though it had already been invented. She gazed at the car. It was useless before, and now it was her most valued treasure. Her *idea* was better than stealing.

The tires! What she saw changed her mood instantly and a feeling of terror swept through her. The tires . . .

were flat. Instantly she fell to her knees and studied the rubber with her hands. Had they been cut? No, she could find no cuts or holes. Why?

A thing like this couldn't just happen. Who would have done it? And why? What could they gain by it? Did they want to beat her to the supplies? Were they jealous? She had brought the car back to life, used it to find supplies. And they had simply and horribly killed it. There was no good explanation. It was evil.

Her mind was filled with so many questions that she barely heard the voice that called to her for the third time. "Lisa, I'm hungry."

"Oh, Todd!" she cried. "They've ruined our car. Look at the tires!"

He walked to the car, and with a calmness and confidence that she hadn't seen in him before, examined the tires. Then, without speaking, he walked to the garage and returned with the tire pump. "Here," was all he said.

They fumbled for a time before they were able to attach the hose to the valve on the tire. Lisa and Todd took turns pumping. It was very hard work, but before long, the car stood proudly as before.

"Todd, you're a genius!" Her words brought a wide grin to his face that stayed all through breakfast.

"I'll do dishes this morning," she rewarded him, "if you'll start collecting some things for me. Today we're going to fix this house up so that all the gangs in Glen Ellyn together can't get in."

In response to Lisa's commands from the kitchen, Todd was an efficient worker, gathering their supplies—hammer, saw, thread, rope, tin cans, cardboard, razor blades, and crayons. He heard her break a drinking glass and he laughed.

The first project of the day was to make an alarm

system. Lisa explained that it would be "logical" to start with that, since it would warn them of trouble even as they worked. "Get the thread, Todd. I'll get some coat hangers."

He was puzzled and asked, "What is 'logical'?" The big word interested him. After all, as "captain of defense" he should know such grown-up words.

"I'm not sure how to explain it," she answered. "Lots of times, when you read a word in a book, or hear it said together with other words, it makes sense, even though you don't know what it means exactly. It seems to fit, but you can't explain it by itself. I think that 'logical' means. . . ." She paused to ask him for the hammer and began to pound a nail into the Harrises' fence.

"I think that 'logical' means that things fit together right. Like in a puzzle, you can't put a piece in wrong, or like. . . ." And while searching for a better example, she tied the end of the thread around the nail.

"Things work a certain way. If you do things right, it's logical. When the tires were flat, I just stared at them and, of course, that didn't help. It wasn't any more logical than crying or kicking the car. But you got the tire pump because you knew they needed air. *That* was logical!"

Her explanation satisfied him. He nodded as though he understood, his curiosity turning to their work.

Without much more conversation, they proceeded with the alarm system. From the nail on the Harrises' fence, Lisa strung a heavy black thread between short stakes made from coat hanger wire that formed a ring around the house. Anyone approaching would catch the thread just below the knees.

Next, on each side of the house, they ran threads through small holes in the windows. Inside they hung a tin can over a carefully arranged stack of cans on each window sill. When an intruder broke the ring of thread, the hanging can would fall, toppling the other cans. The sound would be the alarm.

It took several hours to complete the job—they were both quite clumsy with tools. Lisa, it seemed, spent most of the time just thinking about what to do next.

When it was finished, they stood on the sidewalk to inspect the alarm. "Good work, Toddy-boy. You can't detect a thing—the thread is almost invisible. Now let's see if it works. Todd, you go inside and stand by the living room window and listen. But don't touch anything. And Todd," she called after him, "watch out for. . . ." But it was too late.

Eager to watch this amazing creation work, he ran toward the house. His legs caught the thread, breaking it and setting off a loud clatter in the living room. Sheepishly, he turned to her and surprised her by shouting, "That was not logical!"

Lisa laughed at the word "logical." "Either I'm a good teacher, or he's a smart student," she thought to herself and laughed again. "But our alarm is logical," she called back. "It works! I could even hear it from the sidewalk!"

They reset the front alarm and repeated the test on the other three sides of the house. After some minor adjustments in the back, the work was finished.

During lunch, Lisa briefed him on the afternoon's work. First, they would make warning signs that would read: PRIVATE PROPERTY. DO NOT GO BEYOND THE SIDEWALK. TRESPASSERS WILL BE SHOT. Next, they would remodel the inside of the house to make secret supply storage places. And she described a series of booby traps that they would make. Todd listened carefully.

"The alarm system and the other things will be your

responsibility, Toddy-boy. You must be sure to check them every day. They must be working at all times." Her words made him feel important.

They set to work and, by four o'clock, most of the plan had been accomplished. On the roof in front and back they had rigged large boards behind which were piled rocks and glass bottles. If an enemy approached, Todd was to pull a wire in the house that released the boards, causing an avalanche of stone and glass to roll down on the invaders.

For good measure, Lisa added a small note to the bottom of each warning sign:

> P.S. If you are not friends with our German shepherd, Barney, please wait by the bell cord so we can put him inside.

She thought it was a good finishing touch. They put away the tools and went into the house to write the invitations for the militia meeting.

Her message was simple. She wanted to create a neighborhood militia for protection against the gangs. She hoped that the neighborhood children would bring ideas to the meeting and that all would attend. The meeting would be held in the street in front of the Harris house at two o'clock, Friday. In the invitation, Lisa promised special refreshments.

As Lisa approached Julie's house to deliver the first invitation, she felt a new sense of excitement. It was almost as if she were going to meet a new friend. Since the last, and most terrible, days of the Plague, children had had no time for play.

From the day that Lisa had moved to Grand Avenue, six years before, Julie Harris had been her closest friend. But for weeks now, their friendship involved no more than an occasional wave between bedroom windows.

Charlie answered the door. "What do you want, Lisa?" His tone was rude.

"I want to talk to Julie," and she wondered why he was so crabby. Maybe being the new man of the house had gone to his ten-year-old head. Or, she thought, maybe life with two younger sisters was too much for him. That possibility made her smile.

"What's so funny?" he demanded.

Forcing the smile away, she replied, "Nothing, Charlie. Will you call Julie? Please."

"She's sick. You can go up to her room." And he let her in.

The house smelled awful and looked even worse. Danny, their English setter, had been living inside with them, and apparently no one bothered to clean up his messes. In fact, no one had cleaned up anything. The kitchen was unbelievable.

Lisa picked her way through the litter and entered Julie's room. She was lying in her bed, eyes open, doing nothing. A book by her side suggested that she had been reading.

"Hi, Julie. What's the matter?"

"Oh—hi, Lisa. I just feel kinda crummy. When I stand up sometimes I get dizzy. I don't know what it is." Her voice was very soft.

Trying to be helpful, Lisa said, "Scott Kopel used to get dizzy like that and he took vitamins because his doctor said his diet wasn't right. You should take vitamins."

Julie glared. It was the same old silly argument they used to have. "Lisa, your family is goofy about pills. Vitamins are a waste of time."

"I know, Julie, that's what your mother used to tell you. But that was when she was here to feed you decent meals. What do you eat now? I think you should. . . ."

The sight of Julie's tears stopped the argument. In an instant Lisa recalled her own words and guessed that the word "Mother" was responsible for the crying.

"I'm sorry, Julie. I was just trying to help."

But Lisa had guessed wrong, because Julie explained in rapid, nervous words that they were actually starving. It was the talk about food that had made her cry. This, guessed Lisa, also explained Charlie's bad mood.

"Charlie has been out every day, but he can't seem to find any food. We've been eating Halloween candy and crackers since last Friday." With a tiny bit of a smile, she added, "I never thought I'd say it, but I hate candy."

"Why didn't you ask me, Julie? I would have helped you. I *will* help you. I'll be right back. Want some soup? I don't have your favorite, chicken noodle, but. . . ." Lisa started toward the door.

"Wait a minute, Lisa . . . . There's something I have to tell you first." Julie seemed a little nervous and she paused awhile before continuing.

"The reason we didn't come to you was . . . well, ah . . . you see . . ." and she stopped again.

"What is it, Julie? What's wrong?"

"Well," Julie went on forcing out the words, "we couldn't ask *you* for help. How could we? After stealing from you? Lisa, I'm sorry. I couldn't stop them."

Lisa was stunned. She felt like slapping her sick friend. In disbelief she asked, "Do you mean . . . that you were there yesterday with the gang that stole our supplies . . . and beat up Todd?" It couldn't be true.

"Not exactly. I was here in bed, but I knew about it

and I suppose I could have stopped them, but I didn't. So I'm guilty . . . and I'm truly sorry, Lisa. Will you forgive me?"

Lisa couldn't answer. Instead she asked, "How did you know about it?"

"The Chidester Gang was in the Triangle yesterday watching you make your trips for food. Tom Logan came to the door to ask Charlie to help steal the things in your driveway. Charlie wanted to join the gang because he didn't think there was anything else he could do. But he didn't want to steal from *you*, Lisa. Tom told him he had no choice. Either he helped them, or he would never get into the gang. So he helped . . . and I knew about it. I'm sorry."

Lisa knew that Julie meant it. "Julie," she said, "whatever you do, don't let Charlie stay with that gang. Nothing gets so bad that you have to start doing wrong things. Don't let him. There are better ways—ways that won't hurt anyone.

"Now I'll get the soup while you talk to Charlie." Lisa added, "By the way, why don't you have food if you . . . they . . . stole all of my stuff yesterday?"

"It's a rule of the gang," Julie answered, "that new members don't share until they've been on three raids. Charlie is supposed to meet them tonight at eight o'clock for his second raid."

Lisa passed Charlie on her way out and said in a tone that made it an order, "Your sister wants to talk to you . . . now!"

"They must have had a real argument," thought Lisa, when she returned with a bag of food. They were still shouting in the upstairs room. The argument stopped when they heard the front door slam.

The moment Lisa entered the room, Charlie began to argue in his own defense. "We need food and I can't find any by myself. I've looked for days. There just isn't any. The gang promised me that we would have food if I joined. I didn't have any choice."

"No choice, Charlie?" Lisa challenged him. "No choice but to steal from Todd and me so you can eat? Do you think I believe that? Maybe," she continued, "if you spent less time feeling sorry for yourself, you would have figured something out. Right this minute I can give you ten ideas about how you can eat till you get old and fat and none of them will mean that you have to steal from anyone. But I'm not giving help to anyone who wants to live by stealing from me."

"But, Lisa," he pleaded, "we were scared. We thought we would die. Julie was sick and there was no food and no one to take care of us. We're still scared. We're starving, you know. It's my job to keep us alive and I'll do anything I. . ."

"Anything?" Lisa stopped him. "Even if it means hurting others? Listen, Charlie, nothing makes that okay. I don't care how scared you are."

Lisa's angry words surprised even her. It wasn't that those ideas were new to her—she had heard them in many ways before. But now she could really understand why they were so important. She and Todd were working hard and were proud to live by their own efforts. When someone thought that his hunger gave him the right to take from them—now *that* was something that made her mad.

"I'm not going to join the gang, Lisa," Charlie promised.

"Sorry, Charlie, but I don't trust you. And I won't give you much help. Not yet, at least. If you want some advice, here it is. There *are* places where you can find supplies. Take my word for it. Spend some time tonight thinking, instead of feeling sorry for yourself, and see if you can figure out where those supplies are. And if you don't want to be afraid anymore, then come to the meeting Friday and we'll make plans that will help us all." Lisa handed him the notice.

"In other words, Charlie, use your head. I know how hard that must be for you," she said sarcastically. "Think . . . and you can take good care of the Harris family." She was finished.

Julie had not spoken. She had been listening, amazed to hear her old friend talk like this—like some grown-up. She wondered how Lisa could have changed so fast.

Lisa wasn't looking at Charlie when she said, "Charlie, there's a bag of food downstairs by the door. I'm leaving it because Julie is my friend." And she left.

Outside, as she delivered the other invitations, Lisa made excuses for Julie. "She was sick and besides, what could she have done?" She knew the answer to that question, but she just couldn't let their friendship be forgotten.

At the Cole's house, on the other side of her own, Lisa found a similar situation. Cheryl was eleven; her brother, Steve, was twelve. The rest of the family had gone with the Plague. They were running out of food and, in desperation, Steve was also planning to join the Chidester Gang. Lisa urged him to wait until after the meeting, sparing him the lecture she had given Charlie.

Craig Bergman was the oldest child on the block. At twelve, he had just missed the sickness. He and his six-year-old sister, Erika, lived in the corner house, at Chidester and Grand. They were doing slightly better than the other children. Craig knew a lot about gardening, and he told Lisa of his plans for the spring. Until then, he admitted, they would have a hard time.

Jill Jansen's house had at least eight orphaned children in addition to her younger sisters, Katy and Missy.

Most of the children were under five. Jill was eleven.

Before leaving, Lisa made the same request she had made at the other houses. "Please think about some kind of neighborhood defense. We must find a way to protect ourselves from the gangs. Bring some ideas and be sure to have everyone in your house come along."

That night the candle was out, but the wax still warm, when Todd asked for his story. It was too late—the storyteller had fallen asleep.

—— **FIVE** ——————————————

The time before Friday was filled with hurried activity. From daylight to dark, Lisa and Todd struggled with the problems of getting food and keeping it. Survival—that's what it was all about now, she realized.

The winter days were short and that had something to do with her harried feelings. Everything would get easier as the days got longer. The thought of spring warmed her inside.

But for some reason, and this surprised her, Lisa didn't seem to get tired of "figuring things out." As each new problem came, its solution seemed easier than the last. She was acquiring new skills and confidence in her ability. She liked the new feeling, even though its identity escaped her.

"The meeting . . . ." Lisa's thoughts became focused on that afternoon. "What can we accomplish?" She had visions of earlier days and their play attempts at forming clubs. "They were really a joke, those old clubs," she thought. They had usually ended in giggles or quarrels over who would be president, and they were forgotten after only one or two meetings. "But the militia meeting is very important, and I must plan for it, make it worthwhile."

Lisa decided to cancel her supply trips for that day and study for the meeting. "Study?" she laughed at herself. "Me, asking myself to do homework?" But she knew that the meeting was very important to all of them, and that the object was to plan a kind of "government" for Grand Avenue—like the Founding Fathers had done.

"The Pilgrims had the same type of problems," she thought. They worked long days hunting and building their farms so they would have food. They had no TV, or electricity, or stoves, or grocery stores. They struggled too. They had to worry about Indian attacks, which were a lot worse, Lisa decided, than Tom Logan's childish threats. The Pilgrims crossed the ocean to be free, and maybe that was better than being pushed around by kings and dictators.

Comparing her life to that of the Pilgrims made Lisa feel better. "What am I griping about?" she thought. "At least I have a house, and canned food, and all that the adults left to us."

Lisa realized that she was getting ahead of herself. First, she and the other children had to solve the problem of survival; that's what the meeting should be about. They needed to plan for food and safety. They needed a militia. That's what the colonists had called it. A militia must be the first order of business.

She also had to get everybody planning for spring gardening. Yes, she would share her ideas about the farms and the warehouses—but not for free. Yes, she would give that information, but in exchange for a militia. . . . They must promise her that first. If they could join together for defense, they would be freer to plan beyond food for the next day.

But what if they wouldn't agree to a militia? What if they were too dumb to see how important it was? What if they were so worried about food that they promised a militia and didn't go through with it? She had to take

the chance. Then she had a brilliant idea. She knew
how to handle that meeting. She'd found her secret
strategy. She pondered and rehearsed it until the last
batch of popcorn was made. Lisa was ready for the
meeting.

She would bargain for a neighborhood militia to protect "individual rights" on Grand Avenue—though she
didn't fully understand, yet, why it was so important to
be independent of others.

Children were gathering in the street. The Nelsons
left their house. Todd carried a giant bowl of popcorn
and the pitcher of Kool-Aid. Lisa brought the paper
cups. She also had a large canvas bag tied at the top.

From the beginning, Lisa knew that this would be
different from the old "club" meetings. These members,
all under twelve years of age, were just as serious as the
Pilgrims in Plymouth had been. They seemed to have
some vague idea that their lives were at stake.

Lisa, especially, understood the importance of the
meeting. Her strategy was ready.

The children formed a restless, eager line for their
share of popcorn. The Kool-Aid washed it down.

When the treat was gone, Lisa sensed a good climate
for the meeting and she began. "Yesterday Todd was
beaten up and we were robbed by the Chidester Gang.
Tonight you too may be beaten up and robbed.

"I called this meeting because I think we need to figure out a plan to protect ourselves." She paused to let
the message sink in, and then she continued. "I think
we need to have a volunteer army to protect our freedom. The Pilgrims called it a 'militia.' If we each have a
signal, like the Harrises' bell, to warn us that someone is
being attacked, then we can all join together and scare
off the gang. One person could stay in each house to
guard it, but all the others would come to help the fam-

ily being attacked. Every house would have a different alarm so we would know where to go. For our house, Todd can blow a blast on the trumpet. You could each figure out a loud signal of your own. One person could volunteer to be in charge of organizing the weapons and making defense plans. Probably an older boy, like Steve Cole, could work out the details and be our 'general.'

"This is my suggestion. Do you have any comments?"

The children were having difficulty recognizing the new Lisa. Her speech sounded rehearsed, but they could hear something altogether new in her voice, and they wondered about it.

For a while, everyone was silent.

Then Craig said, "I think you are excited over nothing, Lisa. Has anyone else been bothered by the gangs?"

No answer.

Lisa wanted to reply but she thought, "No, let them argue it out awhile. Then it will be my turn again."

Charlie said, "I think we should form a gang of our own. None of us has food either. There isn't any, unless we steal it. We're dumb not to make a strong gang ourselves. If we wait, the other gangs will have control and we'll have nothing. Then they'll have us in their power. We'll starve if we just *wait* for attacks. I say we start making our own."

Lisa wanted to say a lot about that, but she forced herself to keep quiet.

"I think Lisa's right," said Julie.

"Ah, Julie," thought Lisa. "*Now* I forgive you."

Steve had been nodding approval to Charlie and now he spoke. "The fact is that we don't have *any* food and, as Charlie says, there isn't any except what belongs to the rich kids. Their parents had pantries filled with canned things that they'd never eat. Yesterday I saw Janet Lester swimming in her pool. I'll bet she's got all kinds of extra food. Why not get it before Chidester does? It's not fair. Why should they have all that food, while we have none?"

Lisa thought, "Well, there are two 'generals' we can't trust—rule out Steve and Charlie." But still she kept silent. She waited for Jill to speak. She respected Jill.

But Craig spoke instead.

"I've been thinking that we should grow food. We can do it now; we don't have to wait till spring. I'm making a solarium. It's like a greenhouse and we can raise vegetables in it, even in winter. We can live on vegetables. I know, because my dad told me about vegetarians—they never eat anything but vegetables. We can raise enough to get by."

"Now we're getting somewhere," Lisa thought. She urged him on silently.

But Jill spoke. "So what if you raise food. Are you going to share it with us? If your crop is bad, who gets what little there is left?"

"We do, Erika and I. But why can't you do the same? I don't mind teaching you how. With all those kids, you have plenty of garden tenders."

The discussion was leaving the subject of the militia. Someone suggested that they build a church. "My mother told me, before she died, that the Plague was a punishment from God. I think we should pray and not fight. God doesn't like bad things like fighting. If we pray to Him, I think He will help us find food and maybe He'll even make the gangs leave us alone."

Someone else said that they should try to make friends with the Chidester Gang.

And someone else thought it would be a good idea to hire Tom Logan's Gang. "We can give them food from your secret supply places, Lisa, and they can protect us. Why should we go to all the trouble of making our own militia?"

Lisa just had to speak now. "*We* can use *my* supply? *My* secret supply? Oh, that sounds like a great idea. No thanks, I will decide what's done with *my* supplies! You don't mind, do you?" And she was mad again. It was time for her strategy.

"You're all worried about food. You say there isn't any, so you want to start a gang of thieves or build a church. I could tell you lots of other things you're going to need besides food. How about aspirins? Band-aids? Soap? Matches? Flashlights? Charcoal? Toilet paper? Bactine? Vitamins? Seeds for your solarium? Where are you going to steal them when every child-family has used their supply up? What good will stealing do, then or now?"

Lisa reached into her bag and pulled out a sample of almost every item that she had named. Then she pulled out a Coke. "Who wants one of these?" And she pulled out a handful of candy bars. "Who wants these?" And she threw ten packets of vegetable seeds on the ground—carrot, corn, pumpkin, beans, and some others. She had shown enough. Their eyes were wide as they looked at the treasures.

"I know," she continued, "where to get hundreds of each of these items. My house is filling up with them. And it's not because I'm lucky or because I'm some kind of special person. And it's not because I'm a fighter. It's because I decided to use my head instead of crying or forming gangs of thieves!"

She wasn't finished yet. "But I'm not sharing a thing—not a single thing. You can attack me if you want, but I'll burn it all before I'd let a bunch of thieves have it. . . ."

Her plan hadn't included getting angry. Lisa relaxed her voice. It took a moment. "Craig is right. Soon we can survive by learning how to grow things. Until then, my sources will keep us alive. But I won't share a thing until we have a unanimous deal for a militia.

"For Craig's garden to grow or my ideas to work, we have to have protection against the gangs. They will soon run out of things to steal, and they'll come after us. If we're smart, we'll be growing food and making things, and we'll learn how to survive forever without taking from anyone. But we need a militia, and it will give us time to use our heads. I'll share my knowledge with those who will support the militia."

She was finished. It seemed that her strategy was working. No one had any criticism.

"Any more discussion?" Lisa asked, knowing that there would be none.

"Then," she added, "I call for a vote. All those who promise to support the militia, come over to me. Those who refuse, walk toward the Triangle."

They all came to Lisa. And it was agreed.

"Craig will be commander of the militia," Lisa said. "We will meet here again tomorrow at four o'clock, and Craig will present his plan for our defense. I'll help you, Craig. I have some ideas. Anyone else who has suggestions, please give them to Craig before the meeting. Also, will each house decide on an alarm and tell us tomorrow?"

That was the end of the meeting. One of the children asked Lisa if there would be popcorn tomorrow. She smiled and said that there would be.

The Grand Avenue Militia was formed.

• • •

Lisa's mind was alive with ideas that night. Somewhere in the middle of her thoughts, Todd interrupted. "What does strategy mean, Lisa?"

She was too tired to be sure, but she answered, "Strategy is a plan for action that you think will work. If it does, it's a plan that is logical."

The word "logical" helped make it clear to him, and he asked, "What was your plan at the meeting?"

She explained about bringing the popcorn to gain the children's confidence. And about letting them run out of words and then making her deal—food in exchange for a voluntary militia. And finally, to convince them that she wasn't just talking, she had shown what was in the bag as proof.

"To be free, you need protection against people who want to control your life. No one should tell you how to work or take what you have earned." But she was too tired to say anymore.

"Good night, Toddy-boy. Tomorrow will be a busy day." But before she put her thoughts to rest, she remembered something else that was important.

Ever since the Plague, she had been ignoring her friends and neighbors. She and Todd had created their own private world, and she could see, now, how dangerous that could be.

"They don't all see things the same way I do," she thought. "And I must keep more in touch with them or I could lose everything I've worked for."

She recalled Charlie's comments—and Steve's, and Jill's. What they had said proved that her ideas weren't obvious to everyone. That the Chidester Gang would steal and that her best friend would have a need to deceive her—these things were proof to Lisa that she needed to be a part of their society. Or at least to keep her eyes and ears open and help to build their community into one that could protect her freedom.

"All the brilliant ideas in the world will be useless if that world collapses around me and I'm the only one left to steal from."

Lisa had to start by trusting someone.

"Will you ride with me for supplies today, Craig? We can talk about the militia as we go." He made no comment. "Oh, and you can bring a list of things your family needs because I think we're going to find a gold mine today. I mean a place filled with all kinds of supplies—almost everything we need."

She had used the right words. He agreed to come. "See you at nine."

She approached Craig, who was waiting nervously by the car. "What's the matter with him?" she wondered. He didn't seem to notice her at all. His eyes were fixed on the scratched and dented body of the Cadillac.

"That poor car has been through a lot," she admitted, "but I'm a pretty good driver now, you'll see!"

That wasn't quite enough to reassure him. "He is probably thinking some snotty things about women drivers," Lisa guessed, when, from the corner of her eye, she caught him struggling to get his seat belt on. "I'll show him!" She invested every ounce of her concentration into guiding the car safely and smoothly out into the street—not a scratch!

"Still worried about my driving?"

"Just take it easy, Lisa!" Some of the paleness had already left Craig's face.

"I have one source of supply already that's pretty good. It might have enough food for the whole block to live on until spring, but I'm not sure." Lisa was speaking of the farms on Swift Road. "But today we're going to check out another idea I have. If I'm right about it, we'll find a real treasure—food and supplies to last for years. There might be other important things there, too, like medicine and tools.

"But first, Craig, you have to promise to keep my idea a secret—an absolute secret. You can make use of the secret places to get the supplies you need for your family if you help me on my trips. I want to be the one who decides about sharing it with the other kids when I'm sure they'll actually support the militia. Okay?"

"Okay, but tell me where we're going. I can't leave Erika alone too long . . . and please slow down, Lisa, you just about hit that telephone pole!"

"Big baby," she thought to herself. "I wasn't even close to the pole!"

"Well . . . today we're going to try to find . . ." She hesitated, still not trusting him. "Do you promise, Craig, to keep this a secret? No matter what happens?"

He agreed and she trusted him. After all, what choice did she have? She couldn't make the supply trips alone very easily. Besides, it wouldn't be safe for her to be away so much. With help, she could cut the time of each trip in half. And it would be nice to have a boy along for protection . . . even if it was Craig.

An important thought came to Lisa. "There's one other promise I'd like you to make, Craig. If something should ever happen to me, please promise to take care of Todd. It's a fair deal. My secret places can give you food to keep alive. All you have to do is keep my secret and be responsible for Todd if he ever needs help."

"Sure, it's a deal. I'll be your insurance policy for Todd." They both smiled at the curious thought, and Craig added, "Now, please tell me about your big idea."

"Okay . . . we're going to try to find the Jewel Grocery warehouse on North Avenue. If my thinking is right, it's full of millions of things we need. Don't you agree that if any place has lots of food and supplies, it would be a grocery warehouse?"

"Yes, I think you're right, Lisa. It's a great idea! But what made you think of it?" He meant this as a compliment.

"I don't remember exactly," she answered.

"Watch out, Lisa!" His warning came in time, and she swerved to avoid hitting a stray dog.

They kept driving east toward Elmhurst, slowly and in silence. They both looked out at the streets they passed. There was nothing. No sign of life except a few stray animals. They wondered where the children of these neighborhoods had gone. Had they all moved out? The stores and factories along North Avenue were deserted.

What kind of life did those children have now? How were they learning to survive? Someday, when things were more secure, they might venture in for a look, but not today.

At Highway 83, Lisa and Craig stopped to study the map. Above them stood the colorless face of a traffic light.

From the road, it was hard to read the numbers on the buildings. The fact that the warehouse would have a large "Jewel" sign painted on its front didn't occur to them, until, happily, they saw its large blue letters. They had finally arrived.

To Craig's surprise, Lisa drove past the building and turned into a side street. She explained that it was important to hide their discovery by circling around on the back roads to the rear of the building. The moving car would attract attention for sure, and it would be stupid to lead the gangs to her treasure.

Her heart sank, and she almost cried at the sight of the warehouse. Its broken windows seemed proof that she hadn't been the first to think of the idea. "Not so smart after all, are you," she chided herself. Her confidence in the future faded. Angrily, she turned the car away.

"What are you doing, Lisa? Aren't you even going to look inside, after coming all this way?" But she kept driving. "Stop, Lisa. Go back. We should at least look!" She glared at him for a minute.

Then she said, "Sorry, Craig. You're right. I guess it would be dumb not to look at least. We'll go back."

"Look at that building over there, Lisa. It's just an old factory and *its* windows are broken too. Maybe some kids just had fun breaking windows and never bothered to look inside. The doors are still shut."

She whipped the car around and shot back to the warehouse. Before Craig had unfastened his seat belt, Lisa was running toward the door of the building. It was shut tight. Good! And there was no sign of entry at any of the lower windows. Good! She picked up a large brick and ran along the outer wall, toward the nearest window.

"Wait, Lisa!" Craig's shout followed her. "Don't break in *there*. The wide opening will just make kids curious."

"And don't *you* shout," she said, and she put her finger over her mouth.

When he caught up with her she said, "Okay, how

about one of those windows over there behind the
bushes?" He nodded and soon they were smashing away
at the glass of the large pane.

"Now go to the trunk of the car, Craig. Here are the
keys. Get the box of tools. We're going to have to saw
through these bars."

Craig was impressed with her collection of tools and
even more impressed with the fact that she had planned
ahead so carefully.

The children sawed vigorously at the hard steel bars.
While Craig was sawing, Lisa gave him an account of
what seemed to be inside of the building. "I see rows
and rows of big boxes. I can't tell what they are, but I'm
sure no one has been inside. . . ." It took at least an
hour to cut the main bar in two places.

Craig slipped through the bars first and then helped
Lisa.

What treasures they saw! It seemed that everything
they would ever need was in there. At first they walked
in silence, not believing their eyes. They found more
than just food. There were tools, books, medicines, clothing, matches, candles, charcoal, flashlights, paper
plates, can openers, soap, and much, much more.

For the next hour they wandered through the giant
aisles, their flashlight beam piercing the darkness ahead
of them. They would never forget that hour—ever.

Soon they began to run from row to row. "Craig,
look . . . over there." And he saw a hundred, no,
maybe a thousand cases of canned pop—stacked all the
way to the ceiling. Lisa thought about all of the cooper-
ation she could "buy" with those cans.

"Craig, come here," and they played a game trying to
guess how many jars of peanut butter were in the stack
of cases near the loading ramp.

"I didn't think there was this much soup in the whole

world, Craig. Hey, I've got a good deal for you. You can have all the cream of asparagus and I'll take care of the chicken noodle." Much to her surprise, he agreed. "Weird kid," she thought, "he actually must like cream of asparagus soup!"

Looking at all the food made them hungry. "Here, Lisa," Craig said, and they shared a can of pears. She brought some potato chips from a huge stack of boxes, each holding a dozen packages. They made a meal of pears, potato chips, and warm pop. Craig opened a second can of pears. It was a sloppy kind of fun, eating them with their hands.

While they ate, they talked about the potential of the Secret Place, and by what means they should move the goods to safe hiding places. Above all, they must keep it a secret. Craig fully understood now how important that was.

Lisa summarized their plan. "Okay, we'll take all the canned goods, and I mean every single can. They will last a long time, at least a year, I'm sure. Don't you think so? Breakfast cereal and boxed-up stuff like powdered milk can't last forever, so we'll take only enough to last till spring."

She continued. "We've got to find several different places to hide the supplies in case any one storage place is discovered. We'll put a supply of each item in each place."

They decided on six basic hiding places where other kids were least likely to go—an empty hangar at the DuPage County Airport, the old silo at the farm on Swift Road, the basement of Cottington's Furniture Store, and the furnace rooms at three churches in Glen Ellyn.

But as their plan unfolded, the fun and excitement began to give way to the reality of the hard work, and

the danger, that lay ahead. They knew that their count-
less trips would have to be made at night in total darkness—no car lights on the long drive down North Avenue. It seemed a frightening thing.

"Lisa, the militia meeting starts in one hour. We'd
better get moving." They rushed to load the car with the
things they'd never expected to have again—chewing
gum, and flashlights, and marshmallows, and popcorn,
and pop, and candy bars.

"You drive home, Craig," Lisa said, as she climbed
in the other side of the car.

The challenge frightened him at first, but naturally
he tried not to let it show. To make it easier for him,
she said, "The way I learned was by remembering the
instructions my dad gave over and over when he taught
my mother how to drive. He said them so many times
that I learned them by heart."

Lisa began to recite the instructions while Craig
guided the car slowly and clumsily out of the warehouse
lot. "Look all around you . . . release the brake . . .
easy on the gas. . . ."

The car shot forward and ran over a trash can next
to the warehouse. "So," Craig thought, "that's what she
meant by 'easy'." It did no real damage to the car, just
another dent in the right fender. "This beat-up car is
indestructible, a wonderful thing left from the old
world," he said.

As they drove away, Lisa looked back, not wanting
to lose sight of their new treasure place. In her eyes
now, the warehouse seemed ten times larger than when
they had first discovered it.

The two children rode for a long quiet time, not noticing the November grayness. Their thoughts were filled
with happy images of the Secret Place. That warehouse
offered security—an end (for a while at least)—to their

struggle against starvation. If they were smart—and careful—at moving and hiding the treasure, they would have the luxury of a whole year to plan for the future.

Craig was a natural driver and Lisa told him so. At first she had wanted to get even with him for his "back-seat driving," but she knew that it was wrong to tease him now. Besides, he was fun to be with, and, together, they would have a better chance.

She laughed when, in needless panic, he slammed on the brakes and the front seat filled with pop and marshmallows. "Easy on the brakes," she said, repeating her father's words.

Craig was the only "child-man" she knew. She understood his life and his fears, because they were the same as her own. It was good to understand someone that way.

North Avenue was still deserted as they moved toward home. "Where are the children?" they wondered again to themselves.

Craig wanted to know about Lisa's other source of supply. When she explained about the farm on Swift Road and the inviting note from the old lady, he became interested.

"You know, Lisa, if I could choose any kind of life in this mess, I think I would want a farm. Growing things is such great fun. Let's go to that farm sometime. My father taught me a lot about gardening and I know that I could raise food. Wouldn't it be nice to stop looking for food and start making it instead?"

Lisa thought a long time before answering. "Somebody has to grow food, that's true. But, Craig, do you really want to hide away on a farm? The *real* fun is in planning and getting the world back to the way it was, with schools, and hospitals, and electricity. Don't you see how important those things really are? What good is it to dig in the dirt all day when we could learn to get those exciting things working again?"

She paused, expecting him to say something.

"Just think of the big jets sitting on the runway at O'Hare Airport. Once they carried people away to beautiful places, and now they just sit there. We have been spending whole days trying to find food. Now that we've found a big supply, let's try to figure out a way to get things working again. I mean the jets and trains and things. . . ."

"Lisa, you're a dreamer. Don't you know that it takes years of training to fly a jet? Besides, there aren't any teachers left and the knowledge is gone with them. Books can't even teach us. Forget about it, Lisa. Face up to it—we're only children."

How could she answer him? What could she say? He was probably right, but would they have to live like the people in olden times, spending long days in the fields? Or even worse, would they have to live like those children in really poor places, begging, stealing, and having no time for play? Would they grow old and tired while the jets on the runway rusted and died forever?

"Craig, I know it sounds crazy, but I think we can do it. We can make things work again. Sure, we're just children, but . . ." and her words, like her confidence, faded into confusion.

They drove without speaking from North Avenue to Swift Road, to St. Charles, Riford, and then turned onto Grand.

The children were waiting in the street for the militia meeting and their popcorn treat. Lisa and Craig saw them and what they really were as the car moved to its place in the driveway. Those children were not children any longer, and for a fraction of a second, they both knew that they *were* capable of making a new life.

SEVEN

"This is not my meeting," thought Lisa, grateful for the fact that Craig was in charge. She was feeling too confused to be a leader.

Craig described his careful plan for the Grand Avenue defense. Lisa alone could see that his heart wasn't really in what he was saying. His love for farming and his need for peace and simple things were a strange contrast to his talk of defense and war.

The other children were listening carefully. Craig had a plan that made them all feel safe. Tomorrow they would begin the work. They would set up a different alarm system for each house, and from the Glen Ellyn Police Station they would get guns and ammunition. They would make bombs by pouring gasoline into glass bottles; each house would have a loud watch dog; they would have knives, rocks, and other simple weapons.

The children were no longer afraid, and when they learned of the fantastic treasure in the Secret Place, they were joyous! Everything was going to be all right—they just knew it would. Nobody would dare attack the security of Grand Avenue, and they believed in Craig's plans.

Lisa studied their faces. "Look what Craig has done for them," she thought. "Erika looks as happy as she did on her last birthday. Even Julie is smiling. . . ."

. . . And finally her eyes came to Todd's face. But it had an altogether different look. He was staring down the street and turning pale. He pointed toward Chidester. She turned to look. . . .

. . . The Chidester Gang! There must have been fifty of them, mean-looking, and moving slowly toward the happy gathering.

A few of the children screamed and ran away. The meeting was over.

"Wait!" Lisa ordered. "Stay here and we'll see what they want. Don't run away! Don't look afraid!"

The mass of the gang stopped and their leader, alone, walked forward. "Lisa Nelson," he called out, "I want to talk to you."

She stepped away from her group to meet him. "What do you want?" she asked, sounding calm and strong.

"I'm Tom Logan," he said, "and I've got a deal for you." He didn't look at all afraid.

"Say it," Lisa replied with a fearlessness that matched his.

The children watched.

"I know that you've got all kinds of supplies. We don't know where you're getting them yet, but we'll find out—soon." He was threatening her.

"We could wipe you out, right now, and take everything you have, but we don't want to do that." He paused to make his threat sound more frightening. "But we don't want to do that," he repeated. "You have the supplies and we have the army. I want to make a deal. We'll protect you with our army if you'll share your supplies with us."

Lisa said nothing and waited.

"There are other gangs, you know." Tom Logan was growing impatient. "Those gangs are strong too, and to-

morrow—or tonight—they could wreck you. You need
help, and we'll give it to you in exchange for a share in
your supplies."

Still, she said nothing.

"Lisa, my sister was your babysitter for two years.
She liked you, and I like your family, too. We should
cooperate. We can. . . ."

It was as though she was waiting for him to say
something else.

". . . Okay, Lisa," he said finally, "I'm sorry for
what we did to Todd, but we had no choice. You can't
run a gang without food. My boys were starving. I *had*
to do it."

Now she understood him a little better. "Sorry, Tom,
but I could never trust you, or your gang. If you would
betray a neighbor once, you'd probably do it again. At
least I'd never be sure."

"Now wait a minute!" Tom started to defend himself, but it was still Lisa's turn to speak.

She went on. "We can take care of ourselves! We
have supplies, you're right, more than you could ever
dream of. And soon, we'll have power too—a militia
that could stop your gang any day. Go ahead. Take our
things. You'll waste your time, because today there's
not much here for you to steal. But by tomorrow and
the next day, we'll have things that you will never
have—because you're not smart enough to find them
yourself. Just try to attack us. You won't know what hit
you!"

"Don't get so emotional," she cautioned herself.
"Easy." She wanted to hurt him for hurting Todd.

"I don't blame you, Tom . . . really." Her words
softened. "And I don't want any trouble with your
gang. It's just that we don't need your help. We can
take care of ourselves—and we will!"

The children were silent, and they wondered what gave Lisa the courage to say those things.

Tom's confidence was shaken. He wanted to scare them into an agreement, as he knew he could, but there was something about him and her and their neighborhood past that made him walk away.

He said nothing more. His gang followed him back to Chidester.

It took some time for the militia meeting to return to order. No one wanted what the gang offered, but they were uneasy about the threat to their safety. They had food and supplies and a strong plan for defense, but still they worried.

"Anyone want some more popcorn?" Lisa asked, hoping that the old bribe would bring the meeting back to order.

"No thanks" was the general reply. Then they began to ask a hundred questions about the Secret Place and the militia. The people of Grand Avenue wanted to protect their futures. Popcorn was something nice to be saved for another time.

Lisa whispered to Craig, "Are they really just helpless children? And Craig," she continued, "don't forget your promise. They must not know where the Secret Place is."

Craig nodded and thought about his promise. Lisa was something special—a little crazy maybe, but she was *some* girl. "Sure, I'll keep the promise," and he looked at Todd's face. "In just one day I'm the general of an army and an insurance policy for a little boy. This whole day has been incredible!" he thought.

Lisa, even more than the other children, understood the day's importance. "Come on," she hollered above the many voices, "let's go to Lake Ellyn for a campfire. I've got a whole sack of marshmallows and there's pop and potato chips in my trunk. Craig, help the boys get firewood and build a bonfire by the boathouse. You girls go get the blankets . . . and Julie, can you get your Campfire Girls' Songbook? Hey, Todd, give me a hand with the pop."

In a few minutes, Grand Avenue was left vacant for any gang that might choose to attack it. Every child was happily in the procession to Lake Ellyn. The bronze Cadillac led the way and twenty of the happiest children in the world followed it, singing a Christmas carol.

They had almost forgotten about Christmas. It would be coming soon. When Eileen, one of Jill's kids, wondered if Santa would bring presents this Christmas, Lisa assured her that he would. They would have to bring some toys from the warehouse and wrap them for Christmas morning.

"Charlie, go back to your house and get all the Christmas tree decorations you can find." Lisa surprised him with this order. It was still a little early for Christmas, but he did as she asked.

They built a huge fire near the lake.

Charlie followed the sound of the singing and set the box of ornaments down as he approached the gathering. "What do you want these for?" he finally asked.

"What do you think, dummy? We're going to decorate a Christmas tree." Lisa carried the boxes to a pine tree near the fire.

The children were fighting over the decorations. "Wait a minute. We can't all do it. Katy and Toddy will decorate the tree."

They sang all the Christmas carols they could remember—and that was a lot, because Julie had a fantastic memory for songs. They sang "Frosty the Snowman," "Jingle Bells," "Deck the Halls," and "Rudolph the Red-Nosed Reindeer." The marshmallows were gone in no time, and the children were happy. The fire was huge and bright. They laughed and sang and forgot about tomorrow's problems.

It was like the parties in the old days. Tonight they were children again. Life, as they saw it at that moment, was truly fun.

Charlie, who had been more afraid than anyone, began to act like his old, mischievous self, teasing his sisters and making them mad. Even that was fun, except, of course, for Julie and Nancy. . . . The children laughed until very late into the night—they didn't notice the cold.

The moon was full and shining on the icy lake. Lisa wandered toward it to be alone for a moment. There were many problems to think about and this was a good time for thinking. "What will happen to us?" she wondered for the hundredth time since October. But now she didn't fear the answer as much because it seemed that they were beginning to control their own futures. They would use their heads. That was the key, and. . . .

"Lisa, is that you?" called Jill from her dark perch on the dock. "Come here a minute. There's something I want to talk to you about."

Lisa sat beside her. They listened, for a while, to the songs in the background. There was no hurry.

"What is it, Jill?" Lisa finally broke the silence.

"Well, I've got a problem and I thought you might be able to help me. There are fourteen kids at my place now and they eat like crazy. We just don't have enough food or supplies. Lisa, will you help us? We need lots of things, especially medicine. Some of the kids have bad colds. Do you have anything for us?"

Lisa knew that she could help them. In fact she'd be happy to share the wealth of the Secret Place with Jill and her kids. But why should she, if Jill's kids wouldn't help with the militia?

"Okay, Jill, here's what we can do. I'll be happy to help you out, but not for free. I'll need one child for every hour of the day and night to walk up and down Grand Avenue as a sentry to alert us if an enemy approaches. I'll get my dad's trumpet and they can learn how to make a warning blast on it. But I'll need someone night and day—every day.

"And also, I'll need at least two of your kids to help Craig and me on our supply missions. It will take about four hours for each trip, but we'll probably go only three nights a week until January.

"If you'll agree to those terms," Lisa said, "I'll guarantee you and your kids all the supplies you need."

It was obvious that Jill wasn't ready to accept the deal. Her awkward silence made that clear.

Finally she spoke. "But, Lisa, can you imagine what it would be like for a five-year-old to walk up and down Grand Avenue late at night, afraid of everything that moves? Can you imagine how scared they'd be? You and I are older. We can find the courage to do it, but they can't. I think it's cruel of you to demand it of them. They need our help; they're afraid, Lisa. Don't you remember what that's like?"

"Of course, I remember, Jill," she replied, "I'm afraid almost every minute of the day. So is Todd. He's not much older than your kids, but he's proud of his ability to fight that fear. He earns his way and it makes him happy and strong.

"He doesn't want sympathy. He wants to be helpful and brave. My gosh, Jill, you and I are still children, but we have to keep alive. Everything is changed now. Those kids need the same things we do! They've got to *try*, too."

But her arguments fell on deaf ears. Even Lisa, when she thought about it, couldn't expect the helpless children to join an army.

Lisa gave in, finally, but only because she couldn't put the facts together. Was she expecting too much of those children? Maybe Jill was right.

"Okay, Jill, I think you're right. Maybe I expect too much of everyone. But you have to understand the way I feel. I've found that it's not such a bad problem—surviving, that is—but we have to use our heads. In fact it's our chance for real fun in life—when we know we've actually *earned* our survival. We'll have something then. That's the way I felt today when we found the secret supply. But I don't think you really understand what I'm saying. . . ."

To Jill it sounded good, but the facts she faced every day didn't quite fit with Lisa's ideas. To Jill, life was a sad conglomeration of little things—little orphans and the problems of finding food and medicine for them. Somehow, she just couldn't think of those real problems as "fun" or part of a "grand plan."

Then Lisa said, "Sure, Jill, you know that I'll help you. There's plenty for your kids in our Secret Place and you're welcome to whatever you need."

Lisa didn't think much more about the conversation. She knew something was wrong, but she couldn't be sure what it was. Were her feelings so peculiar? Was the life struggle such a sad thing, or was it the key to her happiness, and theirs? She wasn't sure.

But she did realize one very important thing. Her ideas might bring them all a year of freedom from hunger. The idea of the warehouse, and the car, and the farm—all these things were helping to save the lives of her comrades. It seemed to her that they all felt it was her duty to help them—that what belonged to her was theirs also. . . .

"Oh, well," she thought, "they're afraid. I can understand that. Maybe I'm just lucky that this whole madness is a challenge for me."

In the warmth of their bed that night, Lisa tried to explain her feelings to Todd. Would he understand?

"At first, this whole mess scared me, Todd. I was worried about us dying of starvation. It seemed like a horrible thing—working just to stay alive.

"But then the struggle itself began to seem like the best thing I had. What fun would it be if we were robots—if everything was automatic and we couldn' change anything? Just think of a robot, Todd. He can' feel, or choose, or gain or lose. He can't think and he doesn't even know that he exists. Think what it would be like without any problems, Todd. Life would be dull. Sure, we have a lot of problems right now, but problems are really challenges and they can make life exciting, if you're not afraid.

"I'm proud of my discoveries, even though it's true that anyone else could have found them. And that's really true, Todd—anyone else could have done it.

"Todd, are you still awake?" He was and he felt he had understood his big sister. He didn't ask for a story that night. Their life, in itself, was becoming an exciting adventure.

"Lisa," he said, "I'm glad you're my sister."

They went to sleep.

EIGHT

The week that followed was filled with activity. The defense plan was under way and the children of Grand Avenue were excited.

Security was important. They all knew that now, even the youngest could understand. The Chidester Gang would be back and other gangs would try to capture their supplies. They had to be ready.

Julie and her family had the job of training watchdogs. They would fight to kill on command—or at least that's what Charlie promised.

Each child-family had its own defense alarm. Lisa's house would use the sound of Todd's trumpet. Craig's would use a loud whistle, and the children in Jill's house would beat a drum. The Harrises' house was permitted to keep its old family bell. It once had been heard for blocks at dinner time.

While the defense plan was taking shape, Grand Avenue sounded like a machine at work—hammers, dogs, alarms, rock slides, and children shouting. "Hey, where'd you put the hammer?" . . . "Craig, come here! Is this right?"

The sound of gunfire was the hardest thing to get used to. At nine each morning, Craig held target practice in the Triangle. All children over five years old had to come. They fired small 22-calibre rifles at tin cans

lined up along a low branch. Even though he didn't
know very much about guns, Craig was their teacher.
The children all feared that part of the training, yet they
tried to learn.

"It sounds like we're having a war," Craig thought.
He wondered how many curious children would be
drawn close enough to investigate the noise.

Lisa and Todd's idea of a rock slide on the roof was
adopted as a standard defense measure for each house.
Lisa and Todd showed the other child-families how to
set it up with wire hangers and string surrounding the
house.

Craig helped the family captains find bottles and gasoline to make Molotov cocktails. They were impres-
sive, those gas-filled glass bottles. When thrown onto
the pavement, they made a frightening explosion and
burst into fire. Of course, there was no gasoline from
the pumps at the gas stations, but each house had a can
or two for the power lawn mowers. The children filled
old Coke bottles with the volatile liquid.

The militia captains from each house met with Craig
every morning to discuss the day's plans. He was
pleased with their progress. "The Grand Avenue defense will soon be in good order. We should be proud of
ourselves." Craig's praise was mild, considering his ac-
tual feelings for his captains. He looked at the loyal
aides—Jill, Charlie, Lisa, and Steve. Each day, their
cleverness amazed him more. They had many good
ideas, and they worked very hard.

The captains left each morning's briefing with drawings, tools, and all kinds of junk that had no apparent
value. These were the devices they would need for the
day's construction—rope, wire, tin cans cut up in odd
ways, ladders, planks, and saws. Each captain had to

modify the plans according to the special needs of his house.

Craig worked in Julie's basement because there were more tools available there. "Too bad the power saw has no power. It would have saved a lot of work—and blisters," thought Craig, looking at his hands.

Charlie and Todd helped Craig in the shop. They reported for work at six each morning and the three of them hammered and sawed furiously to get the day's devices ready for the captains.

"Darn it," Charlie said, whenever he hit his thumb with the hammer. Craig kept him from swearing because he thought it was bad for Todd to hear it. He would have been surprised to hear Todd's own muttered words when he bumped his head on the work bench for the fifth time in one morning.

It was strange to see the change in the Grand Avenue captains as the days passed. They were collecting bandages and bruises faster than the wounds could heal. There were no major injuries, fortunately. "Hey," Craig laughed, "we look like a real army with all these bandages, and we haven't even had a battle yet."

The Grand Avenue houses were changing slowly into odd-looking fortresses. By the fifth day of their work, there were rock piles on each roof, waiting to be triggered. A system of ropes and pulleys connected one house to the next and a small mail pouch hung on a rope to carry messages back and forth. Mean-looking dogs were leashed at the front and rear entrances of each house. Warning signs were nailed everywhere. Barbed wire from the hardware store was nailed to the trees, forming a barrier around each house. Every window was boarded up. Shutters had been ripped down and nailed over some.

Long narrow planks stretched between the rooftops,

forming a network of catwalks. "In case of a heavy attack," Craig explained, "it will be safer for us to be together in one house. We can climb across the roofs to Julie's. We'll make trapdoors to get inside."

In the evenings, just before dark, the children had militia meetings. They practiced using knives and baseball bats and sling shots and spears. Each child eventually chose his favorite weapon and practiced with it against imaginary enemies. Craig planned various battle strategies and drew maps of the block that he used for plotting their defenses.

All during the week they had emergency drills, like fire drills at school. When an alarm sounded, Craig timed their response to see how fast they could gather their weapons and rush to the house in danger. At first it was a mess, with children running in every direction. But after about twenty drills, they could assemble in less than four minutes.

After the first drill, when they gathered together to laugh at their confusion, Eileen came up with a brilliant idea.

"That was really fun," she said. "It's just like a fire drill at school." And then she suggested, "Why don't we get some fire 'stinguishers' and squirt them at the bad kids? That would be more fun than shooting guns."

What made her think of that? They couldn't imagine, but it *was* a good idea, and Craig sent a detail of children to Forest Glen School to get a few. They worked very well—the shooting foam would at least confuse and slow down their attackers.

The ideas were really working. Everyone on Grand Avenue was having fun with the militia. They were proud of their work, and though it was never actually mentioned, many of them were beginning to share Lisa's feeling that working to survive and feeling proud of it was a reasonable kind of happiness. It seemed that they were building a real community.

Each end of the street was blocked with barbed wire and dogs that liked to bark. A large sign stood by each blockade as a warning to intruders:

WARNING
Private Property.
Travel at your
own risk.

We want friends
and peace. We don't
want to hurt you.

And it was signed: "The Citizens of Grandville."

They were ready, now. They all felt it.

On the sixth day, Lisa and Craig decided it was safe to resume the night supply trips to the warehouse.

"It will be safer to have two cars, in case one should break down," Lisa said. "I'd sure hate to walk all the way back from the warehouse. Do you think you can drive your dad's car, Craig?"

"I'll try, Lisa," Craig answered.

That night, when all the houses were quiet, Lisa instructed the sentry: "Be especially alert tonight. We'll be back by midnight."

The two cars left the blockade slowly, without lights, and the sentry wondered how they would make it. It was very dark; there was no moon at all. He followed them with his eyes as far as he could, until they went over the hill on Riford.

There was a loud crash from that direction and he

ran toward the top of the hill. No sign of anything. He
returned to his station. "They must have scraped a pole
or hit a garbage can," he thought. "I hope no one heard
it and saw them driving away." He turned to look at his
street and rubbed the chill from his hands.

In the front car, the girl's thoughts were racing.

"What a dumb thing to do, scraping the side of that
parked car. I'll bet Craig's getting a big laugh out of
that. Oh well . . . I hope the warehouse is still our
secret. . . . What should we get this trip? Toddy's
been quiet lately . . . maybe I should take him along
next time. It's neat how happy everyone seems to be
now. I hope we won't need to fight anyone. Maybe we'll
look so strong that no one will even bother to try. When
we get all six supply places filled, then . . . then, we
can start to plan for raising food. We'll need to know
more about medicine and first aid. What if someone
gets wounded? . . . I wonder what Craig is thinking
now . . . ." She wished he was with her so they could
talk together.

"There are stray animals everywhere," she thought
angrily, as she slammed on the brakes to let a cat cross
the road.

The screeching sound from behind told her that
Craig wasn't paying close attention to his driving. She
instantly stepped on the gas to avoid his crash, but not
in time. His car struck hers hard and both of them got
out.

"Not too much damage, I guess. Just another couple
of dents. Before long, Craig, your car will look as bad
as mine."

Craig just stood there.

She continued. "Relax, it's no big thing. Just don't
drive so close next time." Craig said nothing. They got
back into their cars.

He was still a little shaken by the accident, but soon his thoughts turned to other things.

"I hope that no one else has found the warehouse. I must remember to look for garden seeds while we're there. What a dumb thing to do . . . hitting her like that . . . . Dad would really be mad if he could see what I've done to the car . . . . I hope we never have to fight anyone . . . . I don't see why I should be in charge of the militia. Fighting is against my nature. It seems to me that building up our militia is just an invitation to trouble. Sure, we say we're doing it just for defense, but who's to stop Charlie from provoking a battle? . . . Maybe Lisa will find another general . . . . I can't wait to see the farm that she talked about . . . . Wow, it would be fun to have a place like that and raise food. It's not that I'm a coward, and I do see that we need some protection, but I think we're getting carried away with the whole thing . . . . Those kids think it's all great fun now . . . play fighting and shooting guns and planning strategy . . . but just wait until they see some of their own blood . . . . Oh, I'll admit it's been fun building some of those traps and stuff, but . . . ."

It was very dark. As they drove, their minds were concentrated on their problems and the days ahead.

"I'll be the general for a little while, until I can train someone else to take over, but who?" And Craig was thinking of his farm.

Lisa's car was barely visible ahead. Now and then her brake lights would flash a warning to him, otherwise, it was dark.

"We don't need to start all over," Lisa thought. "If we look hard enough, I'm sure we can find the knowledge we need to get some of it working again. Maybe not the jets, at least not for a long time, but for sure the power and water and . . . . I don't want Craig to get too serious about that farm. Other children can raise the crops, but I need him to help me rebuild things. He has a bright mind and I'll need all that kind of help I can get . . . ."

There were so many things to be done, important things, like setting up a school and a hospital and keeping peace. Of course, it would all take time, but those were the most important things. Knowing how to raise corn wouldn't help remove a bullet from a wounded child. Cattle would give meat and milk and they would surely need the food, but who was going to teach the frightened children how to survive in an alien world?

Maybe Craig was right. Lisa wished that she could put her feelings into words, but she didn't know the words tonight. Her mind was confused. It couldn't focus on anything but the black road ahead. Something was wrong; Lisa could sense it!

Their eyes became sore from following the faint white dashes painted on the highway. Finally, they reached the warehouse. It hadn't changed.

"Bring the flashlight," she whispered, as though their normal voices could carry over the long distance to the houses of the sleeping children.

It was very hard work, loading all those supplies into the two cars. They were exhausted by ten-thirty, but the work continued for another hour. They had packed only essential items—the things that would save their lives. That's what they had decided. "Potato chips won't save our lives . . . leave them for another time . . . cough medicine is important, take it . . . and get some Bactine while you're in that section, aspirin too, and Band-Aids."

"Don't you think we should bring a few treats, Lisa? How about some Cherry-Ola Cola and Hostess Twinkies?" They found some and added them to the other supplies. There wasn't time for them to have a treat themselves . . . . Lisa wanted to have a talk with Craig, but that, too, would have to wait.

The clouds parted for their ride home and the moon lit the road. They drove ten miles per hour, then twenty. The moon made a happy light and their tired bodies were anxious for rest. They drove still faster.

"Why is she going so fast?" Craig wondered, as the speedometer hit thirty.

The road was positively straight and nothing was in their path. Even the strays were sleeping now.

He wanted to honk the horn as a caution for her to slow down, or flash his lights, but he knew he couldn't take any chances.

"She's crazy," he thought and he let her speed away from him. "She must be going at least fifty. She'll kill herself!"

He slowed down a little.

And then *he* decided to speed up. It was easy to control the car, especially when he stayed right in the middle of the road. He wasn't going to let a girl beat him. "This is a cinch," he thought.

The dial was reaching sixty and he could see her just ahead. His hands were frozen to the wheel. No muscle was relaxed. Pulling wide to the left side of the road, he roared past her at the Main Street—Lombard junction.

She came recklessly beside him at Highway 53 and together they slowed for the Swift Road turnoff. Lisa resumed the lead and they went back to their snail's pace. A straight road was one thing, but the sharp turns on Swift Road were something to be reckoned with.

The excitement of the race was gone in a second when they turned onto Grand . . . and saw the street filled with children.

"What happened?" Lisa asked the sentry.

He told them about the Chidester attack. "They must have heard your crash on Riford. That *was* you, wasn't it? They probably saw you leaving and knew it would be a good time to strike."

"Was anyone hurt?" she asked.

"No," he said, "nothing serious. They hit me on the head and went straight for your house. Todd sounded the alarm and pulled the rock slide cord. The dogs were useless. They just wanted to play. But the rock slide did the job. By the time the other kids answered the alarm, it was all over. A rock from the slide hit Tom Logan and knocked him out. The gang was confused without his orders and they thought he was dead. They carried him away and that was it! It was a lucky break for us, because our militia was a sorry sight. Only four kids showed up right away. I guess they were afraid. Most of them watched from behind trees until they thought it was safe to be brave.

"I watched the gang leave. At first, I was afraid that we'd killed Logan. I don't like the kid much, but still . . . we don't want to kill anyone, do we?

"By the time they got near my station, Tom was able to stand up. His head must have hurt a lot. The gang started to come at me but he called them off."

Lisa's little brother was the center of attention. "Good work, Toddy-boy," they were all saying, in one way or another.

"Three cheers for Todd!" they shouted.

Todd was just glad to see his sister. He told her the story again in a rush of words. Lisa listened with new interest. He wasn't quiet anymore; he was excited, proud, and scared, all at the same time.

"You are a brave boy, Todd. Just think of all you saved. They would have taken everything."

Lisa wanted to ask the other kids what had happened to their bravery. Would they have stayed behind those trees while the gang beat Todd up again? What if that lucky rock hadn't found such a perfect mark?

But she reminded herself of their fear. She could understand.

The Grand Avenue Militia wanted to share the credit. Before long, they were inventing new versions of the victory. The defense system they had slaved for was now the real hero. "It worked!" they shouted. "Our defense plan worked!"

The children were proud and more confident now. "Let them imagine it as they please," Lisa calculated. "Maybe next time the memory will feed their bravery."

She knew that there *would* be a next time, but she was certain also that victory would not be a matter of luck—no, not next time!

They could talk of that tomorrow, but tonight they wanted to celebrate.

Craig brought out the treats. Charlie built a bonfire in the street, and someone tried to make up a song about their "Grandville." Julie saved the effort with the tune from "When I First Came to This Land," set to her new words:

> *When we first came to this land,*
> *We were not such happy men,*
> *So we built a fighting band.*
> *Now we do what we can,*
> *And we call our land*
> *The land of Grand—*
> *Grandville—Grandville.*

They sang it over and over until it actually began to sound like a real song. It ran through everyone's head for hours.

Lisa ended the evening with a special announcement: "Let's declare that tomorrow will be the first holiday in Grandville. Sleep late if you like, but meet by the lake at noon." The roar of approval didn't surprise her. They sang their new song all the way to their doors.

NINE

The melody was still in Lisa's mind as she climbed into bed next to Todd. "You were a brave guy, Toddy-boy. Will you come with me tomorrow night to the Secret Place? I need your help. Craig and I must take turns going, so that one of us will always be on the avenue."

It was the best reward she could have given him. "You mean in the car and everything? Oh, sure, Lisa, I'll come!"

"And there's one other thing, Todd. I'd like to have you try to drive the car. We can practice tomorrow in the Glenbard parking lot."

Todd was the happiest boy in the world. As Lisa drifted into sleep, she could hear his excited chatter.

His thoughts raced for at least another hour. "What time is it? What day is it tomorrow? How many days have gone by since we were left alone?" He couldn't be sure, but it seemed to him that it was a long, long time.

The Grand Avenue citizens couldn't sleep late; it was a holiday. At eight o'clock, a small band of children decided to form a wake-up party. Julie was the first to be called, then the rest of her family, Charlie and Nancy. At the Jansens', they added Jill, Missy, Katy, and their orphans, now sixteen in number. Then they went on to Steve and Cheryl's house. Steve was

angry at first, but the cheerful procession was too inviting, and he joined right in.

The mischievous troop went next to the Bergman
house. "Let's scare 'em," said Steve. They quickly surrounded the house, scratched lightly on the boarded
windows, and on the count of ten, broke into a frightening roar of war cries and giggles.

"You didn't scare us!" Erika lied.

Craig was too sleepy to care. "Aw, go away." he said.

"Come on, let's get Lisa and Todd," someone
shouted.

The Nelson house was more of a fortress than any of
the others, so they decided to walk the rooftops from
Craig's. "Be careful," he warned, as one by one, they
tiptoed across the narrow planks above the houses.
"Quiet, you'll wake them!"

During militia practice, Craig had made them walk
those high planks, "You must learn not to be afraid,"
he had said over and over again, but the children were
still fearful. In the past, some of the younger ones had
cried. The older children had pretended to be brave.
But today they all had courage.

"We'll slip down through the trapdoor, one by one,"
he whispered. "I'll go first and help you in. This will be
a 'quiet' exercise. Remember, not a sound." He opened
the padlock with his key.

It looked very odd—thirty children on top of the
house, disappearing, one at a time, into the roof.
"Amazing," thought Craig, "how quiet they can be
when they want to."

Someone slipped on the trapdoor ladder and said a
very bad word. "Quiet!" was Craig's whispered order.
"Watch your step . . . . and your language, too," he
added.

Eileen giggled a little too loudly at the bad word.

The other children glared her into silence. It was a good thing that Lisa and Todd slept way down in the basement.

All of them were in the attic now. Arms and legs were tangled together in a way that started a wave of whispered giggles. "Is that *your* leg, Erika?" asked Katy.

"No, I don't *think* so," said Erika, and the giggles started again.

Craig scolded them. "This is *quiet* practice, remember, so shut up!"

They tiptoed single file, very quietly, down the stairs, through the kitchen, and down to the windowless room in the basement. No one shouted. Julie knocked on their door.

"How did you get in here?" Lisa asked. Todd's sleepy eyes tried to focus on the sea of smiling faces.

They dressed quickly while the other children gathered supplies for the day. Everything was loaded into the two cars.

"Drive slow," Charlie pleaded, "so I can ride on the hood."

"Hey, neat idea," said Steve, and some of the other children climbed on top of the cars. The smaller ones piled inside. They moved toward the lake, followed by the envious shouts of those left to walk.

It was a great day, and surprisingly sunny for December.

The morning was warm enough for outdoor games. Jill took the little ones to the swings. A group of girls sat by a campfire singing. Charlie, Craig, Steve, and a half-dozen younger boys played football until the sky clouded up.

It turned cold when the sun disappeared, and the whole party moved into the boathouse. Why hadn't they thought of it before? It was perfect. In no time the big fireplace was glowing. They laughed and sang for hours.

"Where are Lisa and Todd?" Someone noticed that they were gone.

"They'll be back soon," said Craig. He'd promised not to tell that she was teaching him to drive the car in the Glenbard parking lot. The way he'd answered made them suspicious, and before long the parking lot was filled with spectators and eager students. "It's not hard, really," some of them bragged. "Toddy is getting really good. Look at him now!" He was still the hero of the day.

Before long, Steve Cole approached them. "It's time for someone else to be the sentry. I've been on guard since noon, you know!" He could see the fun he was missing.

"Here, Steve, want to try driving?" asked Lisa. "I'll show you how." He learned quickly. "Good," she thought. "Soon we'll have six or seven cars running."

After Steve's lesson, she called them all together. "Okay, let's pack up and get home. Hurry, now. It'll be dark soon. Load the cars."

The first holiday was over. "None could ever be this special again," she said, and the children agreed.

After dark, Lisa and Todd made ready for their trip. "Keep a careful eye out tonight," she told the sentry. They drove away, but not on Riford this time. "We can't take any chances," she thought, as they circled around on Elm and Main streets and then back to St. Charles at Five Corners.

Todd was excited as they crept along. He studied the deserted highway and wondered about the Secret Place.

Lisa's old doubts nagged at her . . . . But, no, she didn't want to think about them tonight. Something was

wrong. The day's celebration had really been fun, yet
. . . . She wasn't sure what made her feel so uncertain.

Lisa stopped the car.

"Toddy-boy, do you want to drive for a while?" Before he took over, she explained the instruments on the
dashboard and the rules for night driving.

"Why can't we turn on the lights?" he asked without
thinking, already knowing the answer, and he strained
his neck to see the road above the steering wheel.

"Here, Todd, you'd better sit on something so you
can see." She folded their coats and added the pillow
from the back seat. "There, is that better?"

Lisa coached her little chauffeur. "Easy on the
brakes . . . turn the wheel slowly . . . don't jerk it
. . . . Todd, I said easy on the brakes!" But he was
driving the car. Who would have thought it possible for a
five-year-old boy?

"I didn't hit anything at all, Lisa," he said proudly
when the car was finally parked by the warehouse.

"You did a great job, Toddy-boy." What else could
she say after all her dents?

"Please don't call me that, Lisa." He had not minded
the nickname before. She guessed that he felt too big for
it now.

"Okay, Todd," she promised and from her, at least,
he would never hear "Toddy-boy" again.

He was excited about the Secret Place when he saw
it. He wanted to wander on and on through it with the
flashlight.

"Come on, Todd, we've got a lot of work to do."
And in two hours of lifting, carrying, and packing, the
small boy learned a new meaning for the word "work."

Todd slept all the way home. "It's nice to have him
along," Lisa thought. "The little guy is really strong."

"Todd," she thought, "we were just lucky last night.

The Chidester Gang could have wiped us out. You were a brave boy." She couldn't deny that, but still, it had been luck. "That one rock was luck. It could have just scratched Tom and made him mad. He might really have hurt Todd . . . and that cowardly militia!" She just had to figure a way to make them tough . . . .

As the car turned onto Swift Road, Lisa thought, "No, not tonight. Surely they wouldn't attack again tonight." She reassured herself. "They're bound to think that Grand Avenue will be on a total alert. . . ."

. . . . But she was very, very wrong and what she saw next exploded in her mind.

The giant flames reached high above the trees. From as far away as St. Charles Road, she could see the terrifying glow.

"Todd, wake up! Todd! Todd!"

"What's the matter, Lisa?" He looked up and saw the fiery answer. Their home was a huge torch, burning away into nothing.

And then came the tears. The two children stood shaking silently in front of the home they'd always loved. They cried to themselves, as motionless as statues, while the blazing heat baked away their tears.

"Come on, Lisa. Come on, Todd," the other children said. "Nothing can be done to save it now."

But they didn't hear. They just stood . . . and watched.

"There's nothing you can do, Lisa," said Jill. "You and Toddy-boy come home with me now. We have room. Please?"

"Toddy-boy?" He turned around. "Who said that? My name is Todd . . . Todd Nelson." He snapped out of his trance.

But Lisa didn't want to come back . . . ever. "Why?" was all she could say, over and over, in her mind. "Why?" It was more than just a question about the house. Her confidence and her joy and her wanting to rebuild things were at stake. Her dreams and plans were being destroyed with the house.

She stood there, feeling nothing, through the night. The flames became embers, and the daylight finally shone upon them.

. . . . And Lisa and Todd went to Jill's.

Having things is something, but not everything.

Earning the values for your life is more than just something, it is everything.

TEN

"What's the matter with Lisa?" they all wondered. "She just sits there thinking."

But actually she didn't think much about anything during that next week. Jill took care of them both . . . . And Lisa just sat there, though sometimes she would wander by the lake and other times she'd talk to Todd . . . usually in their bed, at night. But most of the time, Lisa did nothing.

Her thoughts were all jumbled. "I'm such a fool," she said at the beginning of too many private sentences. "I talked about changing things and now things have changed me. I thought I could do anything . . . but look at me now. I made such a big deal out of what I *would* do, and now I'm just another orphan."

Jill was good to her. She was patient. And that's what Lisa needed most of all.

The other children couldn't understand her reaction to the fire. She had faced much bigger problems and hadn't been discouraged. Why now?

Lisa was beginning, vaguely, to form an answer for herself. She wanted to believe in the things she used to talk about. Before the fire, everything had seemed very simple to her. "Why not?" used to be her favorite answer to anyone who questioned a wild plan of hers. When the old problems had come up, she understood

what had to be done and was confident. But now she
doubted her understanding of everything. Most of all,
she doubted her plans and her ability to think clearly
. . . . She doubted herself, and she had lost her confidence. And so she waited, and thought.

Lisa became more and more interested in Jill's children. They *were* interesting. She studied them carefully.
They liked Jill for her kindness. And she really was
kind to them.

But still there was something wrong . . . . They
didn't play as they had in the old days. There was something troubling them. They wandered about a lot . . .
and whined for attention or treats. They wanted to feel
useful. Lisa could sense that by the way they smiled
when they had a new idea. "Jill, let's make a garden.
The flowers would make everybody happy."

And Jill would say, "Yes, we'll do that in the spring
when it's warm."

Once a little boy invented a harmless weapon out of
wood-scraps he'd nailed together, and Jill told him,
"You have a good idea there. Show me how it works."
And she patiently watched him demonstrate it.

But it seemed to Lisa that the children quarreled too
much. There were very few toys, and they fought con-
stantly over the favorites. Even Jill lost her temper now
and then, when her words about sharing were ignored.

"Sharing? Maybe that's part of the problem," Lisa
thought one morning. The idea roused her into action at
last. There were enough toys so that each child could
have at least two or three each, but they all clamored
for the same beat-up "popular" ones. The more Jill told
them to "share," the more they all seemed to need one
particular toy for themselves. "What these kids need is
to have at least one toy they can call their very own."
Lisa gathered the children together and tried assigning

toys. But it didn't work; they still demanded the same old favorites.

Jill came in from the yard. "What's going on in here?" She didn't like the idea that Lisa could change her rules around. Sharing was an important thing. Jill was convinced. She knew it was!

Lisa sensed Jill's annoyance. She wanted to bridge the gap between them but wasn't sure about how to do it.

She turned to the children, "Well, assigning toys isn't going to work, but I think I have a better idea. Listen carefully . . . ."

They listened because they were glad to see Lisa put aside her grief. "I think you should each have a new toy, one that is yours for keeps." They, of course, agreed. "But since there are no more toys here, you'll each have to work to earn one—if you want one, that is." They were all willing to work.

Jill started to interrupt the plan, but stopped. She too was happy to see something other than sadness in Lisa's eyes.

Lisa continued. "You know how important it is for us to have our cars to drive. They are bringing us food and many other things from the Secret Place. But soon we will be out of gas for the cars. We need more and you kids can help us." The children looked puzzled.

"Do you remember how your dads used to mow the lawn? Didn't they start by pouring gas from a can into the lawn mower? And wasn't that can a red-colored one? And don't you think it's probably still sitting in your garage?

"Okay, here's the deal." Lisa's old enthusiasm was back. "I'll have a nice new toy for you if you can each find a can of gasoline and bring it here."

Most of them remembered such cans in their old

homes and some were already running for their coats. "Wait a minute, there's one more thing. We will also be needing more cars soon. If you can bring me your parents' keys, you'll get a very special extra reward. A whole box of candy for you alone, just you. Do you remember what their car keys looked like? You might find them in your mother's purse or on your dad's dresser.

"Now, divide up into teams of two and be careful. If you can't find a gas can in your garage, then try at a neighbor's. Jan, you take Beth . . . Bill and Larry, go together . . . Nancy, will you help Eileen?"

The children had a real project now and they hurried about it. "Where's my boots, Jill?" . . . "Who took my purple scarf?" . . . "I can only find one mitten."

Jill helped them, and with motherly concern reminded them to be careful and hurry back.

After they had gone, Jill turned to Lisa. "They do seem pleased with your idea, but I'm not so sure that we should stop teaching them to share things. Sharing is very important, you know."

"I've been watching your kids for days, Jill. Just watching and thinking about them. They do too much sharing and it isn't working at all. They have nothing of their own—no real duties, no real way of helping. It's nice to share things if you want to, but it's bad, I think, to force people to share, or be nice. Those are things a person must decide for himself. Otherwise it's no good. See what I mean?"

Jill didn't agree, but she avoided an argument.

"You do all the work, Jill, and they hardly help at all. They wander about, whining for something to do, and fighting over toys. You're really patient and good to them, but I think they need to have jobs and things of their own."

Now Jill was ready to argue. "But, Lisa, they're afraid, really scared. You should hear them at night, the bad dreams and all . . . ."

"Yes, I've heard them," Lisa said. "I told you I've been studying your kids. All night long you seem to run from one child to another, trying to soothe them back to sleep. But when do you sleep? You look awfully tired, Jill."

"What can I do?" Jill really did want to know.

"I've told you what I think already. The children are afraid because they have nothing, nothing at all. It was bad enough for them to be orphaned, but it's even worse for them to be without their own . . . uh . . . personalities." Lisa couldn't think of the right word and Jill misunderstood.

"Lisa, they have nice personalities and each one is different. What do you mean?"

"Well, I can't remember the word, exactly, but what I mean is that . . . ah . . . well, I don't think they'll ever be happy if you do everything *for* them. They need to work and be proud of themselves. They need to be able to say to themselves, 'I worked hard and did a good job and I *earned* my toy.'

"Don't you see?" she asked. "And, Jill, it would make your job so much easier."

"Maybe you're right, Lisa, but I still think they're too young and too scared."

Lisa wanted to say something about how she had lost her own fear by being too busy solving problems. It seemed to her that fear was how you felt when you waited for something bad to happen, and fun was what you had when you figured out a way to make something good happen.

She wanted to say those things, but how could she now? She had been a victim of her own fear since the fire, just another one of the scared children that Jill took care of.

"By the way," Jill said, "where are you going to get those toys you promised them?"

"That's simple," Lisa answered. "Tonight when Craig makes his supply trip, he can get some. They aren't really fancy toys, but they'll do. The Secret Place has hundreds of them. I guess we just forgot all about play. Doesn't it sound strange, Jill, to think of playing with toys?"

Instead of answering, Jill asked, "What is the Secret Place anyway, Lisa? It sounds so mysterious. Where is it?"

Lisa wanted to tell her, but she said, "You know I can't tell you, Jill, or anyone else. It's too important to risk having it discovered, and if the Chidester Gang really wanted to find out about it, all they'd have to do is torture someone into telling. The fewer people who know, the safer it is."

"Would you tell if they tortured you, Lisa?" Jill hoped she would say no.

"I don't know, Jill. I really hope I wouldn't."

Lisa was feeling much better now. Activity had brought her to life. Knowing that the children would be gone for another half hour or so, she asked Jill to call a quick meeting of the militia leaders. "Tell them to get over here right away."

Charlie, Steve, Craig, Todd, and Jill faced Lisa in the living room of the "Children's House." "She's back to her old self," they thought, as she rattled off a long list of new militia plans.

"Our defense plan is a joke," she said. "We've got to train those dogs to do more than just slobber on the enemy. And we've got to make our kids tougher. They're afraid to shoot or hurt anyone. Where was our

brave militia when my house was being looted? Were
they watching the flames from behind trees? What if
Todd had been inside? Let's make more Molotov cocktails and use them next time."

Was her audience deaf? They sat quietly listening to
her anger. "Don't sound so violent," she cautioned herself.

And for no other reason than to change the subject,
she started talking about her old plans, the rebuilding
plans, survival schools, first-aid stations, and the other
more fantastic dreams. She herself didn't believe it anymore. As if in a trance, she repeated the old plans me-
chanically, without enthusiasm.

Charlie stopped her. "Lisa, you're crazy! Forget all
that junk, and let's talk about the militia."

His words stung her. Even though she too was giving
up on them, the way he talked to her made her angry.
"Crazy, Charlie? Who's crazy? Shut up, Charlie!"

And she stood up. "Go ahead, big militia captains.
Make your plans!" She stopped herself . . . and then
with meaning, and in a soft voice, she added, "You can
do it. I know you can."

"I'm going for a walk," she said at the door, and left.

She came to the bench by Lake Ellyn. "Crazy?" she
wondered. "Maybe I am crazy . . . or am I just sick?
I feel so tired, it's like I have a sleeping sickness of
some kind.

"But I've got to get control of myself. I've got to face
the problems. Charlie was right about that. Forget the
big dreams, for now anyway, and solve today's problems." Her mind was getting clearer. She listed the real
dangers, but now she could finally see that what they
had to fear was much bigger than the Chidester Gang.
What good would it do to build a twenty-man army and
add more weapons? How would that help when Chides-

ter decided to join forces with other gangs? How would their feeble weapons resist an army of a hundred? It was sure to happen sooner or later. One by one she could see the other Grand Avenue houses burning to the ground. She could imagine the "Grandville" citizens tortured and forced to give up their treasures in exchange for their lives, and finally, with no choice left, they too would have to join that army.

Yes, it was clear to her now. Grand Avenue was impossible to defend. They needed . . . they needed a castle with high walls and a moat, like in the days of King Arthur. "Wouldn't that be nice," she thought.

Her fear was dissolving away. She could see clearly now and her confidence was coming back. "I'll figure something out. I will!"

She walked to the lake past the boathouse, and at the end of the dock, she sat down. "I'll figure something out," she repeated over and over again, as if the words themselves would trigger an idea.

"A castle with high walls," she thought . . . and then Lisa looked up. There it was—right before her eyes. A hundred times she'd looked up there and not seen it. But now it was clear.

Glenbard, the old fortress of a high school, stood proudly, high on the hill. Its walls were tall . . . made of brick, too! The field and the lake were below it, on her side. A steep hill descended to Crescent Boulevard on the other.

It was their castle, all right! Twenty children could defend it against a hundred soldiers, maybe two hundred. There were big rooms for the child-families; there were classrooms for the survival school; and the nurse's office for a first-aid center. There were kitchens, and meeting rooms, typewriters, art supplies, woodworking tools, indoor garages—and who could tell what else? And best of all, there'd be a library filled with books.

"Everything except a moat," she laughed. "I've got it! I've got it!" Laughing and shouting, Lisa ran all the way around the castle and then home to tell the others.

The Jansen house was noisy with activity as she approached it. Little workers were bringing gasoline cans for storage in the garage. "Here, Lisa, I found two cans. Can I have my toy?" . . . "Here's some gas, Lisa, and I found these keys. My dad had two cars."

"Nice work. Put the cans in the garage." . . . "Any more car keys? Bring them to me."

Eileen was crying. "Lisa, I couldn't find any gas, but here are the keys. My daddy never brought the car home since he was sick. Are trucks okay? I think trucks are neat, and they can carry lots of things. But I couldn't find any gas," and she started to cry again.

Lisa didn't care about the girl's tears at that moment. "Trucks you say, Eileen? Where?"

"Oh, my dad's garage is on Geneva Road. It's really big. He made roads. There are dump trucks too, and bulldozers, and stuff like that. Don't you like bulldozers, Lisa?"

The little girl couldn't understand Lisa's serious look and she started to cry again. "I do get the candy, don't I, Lisa?"

"Sure . . . sure . . . sure you will, Eileen. But trucks, wow! Can we ever use a truck! Thank you, Eileen. Thanks a lot. Will you show me how to get there sometime?"

"Uh-huh."

Missy had been watching them intently. She hadn't seen Eileen cry much before this—she was such a cheerful girl. Missy came toward her and said, "I already have my can, but I think I know where another one is. Come, I'll show you."

They ran off happily. "Now that's a *real* kind of sharing," Lisa thought.

As she entered the house, she could hear loud arguing in the living room. The militia meeting was still under way—that was more than obvious.

"It will never work," Craig was saying to Charlie.

"Hey, Lisa," Steve said. "Guess who's got the wild ideas now? You ought to hear Charlie's plan. Tell her, Charlie."

Lisa flopped down on the big couch. "I told you he was the crazy one," she laughed.

But Charlie wasn't a quitter. He described how they could train dogs to fight and kill if necessary. He'd read a mystery story about a man who trained killer dogs. And his dad had a book on training police dogs. Lisa was thinking about their castle surrounded by angry dogs. "It would be even better than a moat," she thought to herself.

Charlie noticed that she was smiling and thought she was mocking his plan. "I'm not finished yet, Lisa," he said coolly. He went on to tell them that German shepherds were the best dogs for the purpose, and that since there were so many stray dogs everywhere, he was sure he could find dozens to train. "Besides, I know a lot about dogs. My dad taught me." Charlie had been secretly training Danny, his English setter. He offered to give Lisa a demonstration.

"That's not necessary, Charlie," she said. "I think it's a great idea. It's better to use dogs for fighting than children."

"And . . ." she decided to shock them, "and they'll be useful at the castle."

"What castle?" All of them said it at the same time.

"You thought my other ideas were wild, did you? Wait till you hear this one!"

They listened more and more carefully as she presented the details of the plan. No smiles, no jokes, just the nodding of thoughtful heads. They could see that Grand Avenue was too hard to defend. The houses were too spread apart, and they had learned a lesson from the fire. They knew that their houses might be next.

She had expected them to argue and say that they hated to leave their homes. But the new idea sounded exciting.

"When do we start?" Jill asked.

"Tonight, of course!" Lisa answered. "There's no time to waste. We'll have to spend many secret nights getting the place ready. Then—I'd say in about five or six days—we can move in. Eileen's dad had some big trucks. We'll figure out how to drive one and then, one night, we'll load all our stuff into the truck and slip it into Glenbard."

They worked over the details of the plan until dark. No one but the six plotters would be told a thing about it until everything was set—no one. In the meantime, Steve could learn to drive a truck. Lisa and Jill could plan the indoor city, and Craig and Todd could keep hiding supplies. All of the activity could take place at night and Charlie could be the temporary defense captain. They all hoped that Chidester wouldn't join with another gang, at least for a while. Somehow they would keep the enemy away. They were a team now and they had a real plan.

There was no crying in the Jansen's house that night. "Could it be," wondered Jill, "that earning their own toys is the reason for it?" Even she rested well.

But neither Todd nor Lisa could sleep. They had far too many exciting thoughts.

Lisa wanted her brother to understand why she was so happy. But how could she say it so that he would understand?

A story seemed the best way. And because she had been thinking of castles and bygone days, the scene for her story came to her easily.

Once there was a tiny kingdom across the sea with knights in shining armor who had lots of adventures. Everybody was really happy. They were busy doing things they liked.

In a huge castle overlooking the sea lived the king and his young son, the prince.

The kingdom was very rich because the king was the wisest man in the world—well, at least in their world. He knew how to be happy and he knew how to make his subjects happy. He was fair and generous, and most of all, he let his people be free.

Now you know from other fairy tales that kings usually made their money by taxing the people in their kingdom. Well, not this king—and maybe that was part of his wisdom. Other kings demanded cattle and gifts and jewels just because they wanted them. And they gave nothing in return. They didn't really think that peasants were as good as royal people.

But this king was really a lot like a smart businessman. He thought of his subjects more like customers than slaves. And since he was wiser than anyone—since he *knew* more than any ten of them put together—well, what I'm getting at is that he sold them his wisdom. When they were unhappy, or when they had a problem, they came to him for advice. If he could solve their problem, which he almost always did, then they would have to pay him. He would charge according to the size of the problem. Advice about farming, for example, would only cost a goat or a pig. But advice about how to be happy was his specialty, and because happiness is the most important thing in the whole world, he charged a lot more for that kind of advice. Usually the people paid with their best jewels or with a year of service as a soldier to defend the country against the other kings—the ones who thought it was easy to get rich by fighting and looting.

The other kings couldn't figure it out. Why was he so rich? It seemed crazy to let the peasants be free and have an army that they didn't *have* to join.

But those kings never saw the stream of people in line to buy the king's advice. He got smarter and richer all the time. And the happier and freer his people became, the harder they worked. The harder they worked, the wealthier they became. The wealthier they became, the more time they had to face and solve their problems. And here was the king's secret: while he got smarter, they got richer, and he could afford to raise his prices.

Everybody got happier and happier and the king couldn't complain because he (and they, too) got richer and richer.

But there was a big mystery about the king's happiness advice. The people swore on their very happiness, *never ever* to repeat it—ever!

Such happiness—it was everywhere. Maybe that's why they called it the kingdom of "real fun"! All the people of the land had real fun doing whatever they did.

Does this sound like too happy a story? Well, even the king had problems—wisdom can't stop them altogether you know.

Everybody was getting happier each day, except one very sad, sad person who became sadder every day. And it troubled the king greatly.

And no wonder he was troubled, because that sad person who got sadder every day was the prince, his son!

Now the king's wisdom just wasn't great enough to deal with this problem. He tried everything to make the boy happy. He gave him horses, and smiling friends to play with, and toys and servants, and not a stitch of work to do. The boy had every reason to be happy. But he wasn't.

And the king was smart enough to know that the sad prince could never rule the land—he was learning neither wisdom nor happiness.

The more he gave to the prince, the sadder the prince became.

Before long, the king himself started to become sad. "I'm not so smart," he said to himself, "if I can't even make my son happy."

When he was nearly at his wit's end, the king decided to get help. He offered a big reward and had a notice posted all over the kingdom.

Whoever can tell me how to make my son happy, shall inherit this kingdom upon my death.

And it was signed: The King of "Real Fun".

But as you might imagine, no one could advise the king as he wished, though hundreds of people tried.

And then tragedy came to the king. In the middle of a night that was sadder than most, the little prince disappeared. He was gone, without a trace.

Things got much worse, in fact, before they got better. The king began to lose confidence in his own wisdom and, of course, business began to slack off.

And finally on one day in the spring of the second year after the prince had disappeared, business was so slow that only one person came to the king for advice. The king could see it clearly now. He was going broke! Pretty soon—and he shuddered at the thought—he would have to start taxing his people.

"I can hold out for another month or so," he thought. "Especially if I move into a smaller place. This castle costs a lot to keep up. Maybe my next customer will have a high-priced problem."

And then a visitor was announced.

"Your Highness, this young man seeks advice about happiness."

"Good," the king thought. "Another customer for happiness advice."

"Step up here, lad," said the king, almost greedily. "What is your problem?"

The young man seemed terribly sad. From his expensive clothes, the king predicted a very high price for his advice. "But what if I can't help him?" he thought. Even the king had lost faith in himself by this time.

"Have you guessed the ending already, Todd? These fairy tales are all very much alike, aren't they? . . . You haven't? Okay then, I'll finish the story."

The young man said, "Great King, your wisdom
has let my father prosper. He has earned riches not
possible in other kingdoms. But can your wisdom
help me? Though I have everything, I am still unhappy. I try to be happy. I laugh out loud to myself. I smile in the mirror. I buy new clothes and
horses and jewels every day, but still I am not
happy." And he cried right in front of the great
king.

The king smiled to himself. "This will be easy
money," he thought. "I'll just give him my usual
happiness advice."

"I will help you," the king said. "But first, do
you swear by the happiness I will show you how to
find . . . do you swear that you'll never repeat
the words I shall now tell you?"

"Yes, Great King. I do so swear."

The king went on. "And are you prepared to
pay the high price for such advice?"

"Yes, Great King. I have a golden ring worth
four hundred goats."

And the king drew a small card from his royal
robe with the happiness advice neatly written on it.
(You see, the king never said the words aloud for
fear that some spy would overhear. After all, it
was a trade secret.)

The words on the card made the young man
smile for the first time in his long sad life. The
words were:

Having things is something, but not everything.
Earning the values for your life is more than
just something, it is everything!

"Remember those words, lad. Get to know and
understand their meaning. Happiness is quite sim-

ple, you know. There's nothing in the reality of the
world that you cannot face. Do not fear! Fear is
the ugliest thing because it alone equals unhappi-
ness."

The king's speech was finished and he asked the
young man for the golden ring.

"May I ask you a question first, Great King?"

"Yes, ask it!" said the king, a little impatiently.

"Why, Great King, should I have to pay for
your advice if your own son couldn't be made
happy by it? What good is your advice? Why
should I give you my most precious treasure—my
golden ring?"

The great king was silent for the first time. He
had always had a wise answer, but now he said
nothing.

"Then let me tell you something, Great King.
Let me give *you* some advice for a change. I think
you need it. Why, you yourself are not happy. I
can see it in your face."

The young man reached into his robe and pulled
out a card of his own and gave it to the king. The
king turned pale when he saw it. It said:

Let your son practice what you preach!
Let your son discover the truth that I already
know: "Having things is something,
but not everything.
Earning *the values for your life is more than*
just something, it is everything."
Let your prince earn *the values for his own life!*

The king said, "Maybe you're right, lad. I gave
him too much. Just as your father has done to you.
And if only I could find my son, I would try your

advice. My wisdom tells me that you are right—
that giving him too much was a great error.

"Find my son and bring him to me! If your advice helps him to find happiness, then you shall
inherit the kingdom and all that I own."

"Your Highness, I *have* found him. He knows
my advice and now he is truly happy," said the
young man.

The king was astounded at those words. And he
knew their truth when he saw the golden ring—the
one he'd given to his son, the prince.

The young man removed his disguise and said,
"Yes, Father. I am he—your son and the rightful
prince of this kingdom. I have earned happiness
and the right to inherit all that is ours."

Needless to say, they lived happily ever after.

Lisa ended the story. Todd was trying to think it
through. He didn't understand it completely yet.

The day had been a bright new beginning for Lisa.
She had passed from sadness to joy. She had made a
real plan for the children of Grand Avenue. And she
had, during the course of her fairy tale, touched upon a
grain of precious truth.

She was happy.

The Glenbard plan worked perfectly. On the night of
January first, Grandville became a ghost town. Its citizens, and their secret treasures, disappeared from the
face of the earth . . . .

. . . Or so, at least, it seemed to the fearful and
cruel army of Chidester *and Elm.*

ELEVEN

The move to Glenbard had been kept "top secret" until the very last minute. None but militia captains had any knowledge of the exodus.

The children were awakened that night by the militia captains and a hushed order: "Don't be frightened, we're moving away to a wonderful new home tonight. If you choose to join us, gather all of your belongings and bring them to the front of Jill's house. But ever so quiet—not a sound!"

The captains had memorized the words. The children had to move as quietly and obediently as they were instructed to do. They were all standing patiently by the truck in less than half an hour.

Forming two lines of workers, they passed their possessions along into the truck from both sides. Soon the truck bottom was filled, and the children climbed on top.

It was a large truck. There was room enough for every person on Grand Avenue. It carried them and their possessions to the fortress in the darkness.

At Glenbard, the same two human chains of workers formed, lifting the belongings back out of the truck, and into the safety of the building.

In the pitch black of the school basement, they were told to remain quiet and listen. Lisa spoke to them. "It's very important that you know some absolute rules. This

is my city, Glenbard. We can all live here in safety, but
we can't make one single mistake. You must follow every
rule or you'll be asked to leave. If you don't like the
rules, then you are free to move back to your homes.
You are not forced to stay here.

"The Chidester Gang and others will be looking for
us—for our treasures mainly. We can't give them the
slightest clue that we are here. For the next two weeks,
we will work very, very hard making the city into a fortress. It will be like a castle and we must build it ever
so quietly. From the outside, this building will look, and
sound, completely deserted.

"Okay, here are the rules for the next two weeks.
Listen carefully! There will be no candles or lights at
any time. You must not leave the building except at
night, and then only if you're sent on a special mission.
You must never go near a window or any place where
you might be seen from the outside. You must never,
ever shout. Always talk softly or whisper.

"If you are building or doing any project that is
noisy, you must do it in the basement furnace room. We
will explain the daily schedule later when we show you
around. Just be prepared for two weeks of the hardest
work you've ever known. There will be no playing . . .
no noise . . . no mistakes . . . until we're finished.

"Then," she said, as if to give them courage, "when
it's finished, we'll announce the new city to the world.
We'll make a lot of noise and we'll celebrate."

The children were quiet for the rest of the night.
Only a few muffled questions broke the silence.

Morning came and sunlight filled their new home.
The children wandered all about, looking at the many
curious sights. Someone had been busy in Glenbard
changing the old school building into the place where
they now lived.

At nine o'clock on the first day, Lisa and Jill took the citizens on a tour of the city. They would live in the upper west section, facing Lake Ellyn. The classrooms had been converted into small apartments, with mattresses on the floor and blinds closed over the windows. Each apartment had a wash table in one corner with a pail of water, a metal pan, soap, towels, and a large mirror. A family name was written on each door.

Jill and Lisa had assigned the rooms, dividing all the children into "families." Jill's adopted children were organized into four groups of four roommates. Jill had a room with her own sisters, Katy and Missy.

The building could eventually hold four or five hundred citizens, maybe even more. But now there were only thirty-five, and they seemed to rattle about in the hugeness of the place. As they toured the indoor city, Jill and Lisa took turns explaining their plan.

"This will be our cafeteria. We'll eat all of our meals here. They'll be served promptly at eleven o'clock and five o'clock each day. Don't be late or you'll go hungry. Julie and Nancy, will you take charge of all the cooking?" They agreed that they would. "Lisa Bowser and Carrie Meade can help with the meals and do the dishes. All right, girls?" And they said it was.

Lisa made it clear that everyone would have a specific job in the city and that there would be weekly meetings to discuss any job changes.

She told them that it was her building. She had claimed it. It was her private property, and they were all welcome to stay. But she wanted it to be clear that everyone would do something to support the city. She wanted and, in fact, needed them with her. But they had to know the rules. Anyone who felt mistreated, of course, was free to leave. Lisa went on.

"Someday soon, we hope to have many other chil-

dren here with us, and that will lighten our work a lot.
For a while, though, it will be very hard work, but we'll
all be safe."

"Here is our hospital," said Jill. "I am in charge of it.
Missy and Katy will be my nurses. Be sure you come to
me if you have even the tiniest pain. We have lots of
medicine and I'm studying hard about first aid and
those things. I will become a real doctor as fast as I
can."

The children peered into the small, white room. It
had two small beds with bright, clean sheets. There
were cabinets of books and, in the corner by the window, there was a big sink and some odd-looking metal
equipment. This room used to be the school nurse's office.

They moved along to a group of three classrooms.

"Here is where you will come to school *every* day,"
Jill said. "For a while, at least, there will be no week-
ends in our city. We know that must sound awful to
you, but we have so very much to learn and we have no
time to waste. But we promise you that there will be
many special fun holidays for those who study and work
hard."

They all sat down in one of the classrooms and Lisa
said, "You must report to class at seven o'clock in the
morning. We'll have juice and crackers then, so that
you don't get too hungry. We'll stop for chores and
lunch from ten o'clock until noon. Then we'll have
classes again from noon until two o'clock. After that,
each day we'll work on building Glenbard into a real
city. There's a lot to be done with the militia, and there
are some new plans that you'll hear about later.

"Craig will be in charge of the school, but Jill and I
will teach some classes too. We'd like Julie Miller and
her roommates to be teachers' assistants during the

work periods. Is that all right, girls?" They nodded and Lisa motioned for Craig to take over the talk.

He didn't like to speak in front of large groups, but he was excited about his new job as a teacher. "It is almost as good as having that farm," he thought to himself. "And it's sure better than being the militia general."

"In the morning," he began, "we'll all attend survival classes—Lisa, Jill, and I will teach them. You'll learn about cooking, first aid, basic farming, camping, and so on. Jill will teach the youngest of you, so if you're under five, you must meet with Jill here in this room. All children older than five will meet with Lisa and me in classroom number three.

"Now, in the afternoon, we'll have special advanced classes. I know it sounds funny, but we all have to start planning for our full-time jobs, and that's what these special classes are for. I plan, with the help of some of you, to design whole courses of training in the following jobs: farming, medicine, teaching, defense, machinery, and building. Other courses will be added later.

"Everyone must choose a job in one of these areas. Your morning teacher will help you decide. The afternoon classes won't begin for one month, so you'll have time to make up your mind. Any questions?" There were none, and Craig sat down.

"Oh, yes," he remembered, "during this week everyone must report to the 'strategy' room after lunch. We've got a lot of planning to do—in defense, especially."

"What is a 'strategy' room?" asked Katy.

"Well, come along and we'll show you," said Jill.

It was a strange-looking room with a lot of blackboards and maps of Glen Ellyn. On the far wall were photos and drawings of the outside of Glenbard. On the

long table, there was a floor plan drawing showing the
inside rooms of the building. It was a view from the top,
showing how the rooms were divided by halls and walls.
On this table map were about 40 toy soldiers.

Charlie was the new militia general.

"Strategy," Charlie began to answer Katy's question,
"means planning. In this room, we will pretend in ad-
vance how battles might go so that we'll be ready to
fight them in the best way. See these play soldiers on
the table? Now, we can pretend that the enemy has entered the building at this door over here." And he
pointed to a place on the drawing. "We'll put these toy
soldiers here to stand for the enemy. To plan our strategy, we can move our soldiers to different places on the
drawing and decide the best way to handle this particular situation. By using the maps, blackboards, and other
things, we can practice hundreds of different strategies."

Charlie added, "Todd Nelson, Steve Cole, Kevin, and
his three roommates will be my captains. Is that perfectly clear?" He asked the question in a military tone
that sounded like something he'd learned from watching
too many war movies.

They all understood. Katy said, "That sounds like a
game. Can I play it too, sometime?"

"War is not a game!" replied the tough new general.

Jill and Lisa led them from the strategy room to the
library. "This library has books mainly for older children, so we're going to take the truck to the Glen Ellyn
library and move all the children's books over here.
Eventually, we'll have six rooms of library space and
we'll move everything that we can get from other librar-
ies. We think it will be the most important part of our
city someday. After the city is built, we can have candles after dark. Then you can come to read during the

evening free time. Oh, and Julie Miller and her room-mates have agreed to run the library."

Next, they showed them the game room, which didn't yet look much like a game room. There were just a few toys, but they promised to fill it by the time Glenbard was finished. Cheryl Cole would be in charge of the game room.

They showed them many other rooms. There were three next to the cafeteria for storing food and two more just down the hall for supplies. There was a special room with huge wooden bars and several padlocks. "Here's where we'll store our guns and bombs and things like that," said Jill.

Later they would prepare other rooms: the automobile shop for fixing cars, the woodworking classroom for building things, and the home economics room for cooking classes.

There were many plans for the city's growth. But, for now, their life would be simple and confined to the main rooms. Defense and food supplies were still the biggest problems. These must be taken care of before anything else.

So Julie and Nancy, who soon grew to hate their own food and the job of cooking, made the first eleven o'clock meal at Glenbard. It was soup and powdered milk.

After lunch, the three leaders, Lisa, Jill, and Craig, organized the others into the first day's work groups. There was a lot to be done. "And there's no time to waste," said the leaders.

Lisa and Jill had done a good job of preparation. Everyone could see that they had spent many late-night hours of hard work. The city already seemed a cozy place.

By six o'clock, the Glenbard citizens had sore muscles, but they were also excited and happy about their new home. "Quiet down now . . . get to sleep . . . no candles!" Lisa made an inspection of the family rooms. It was real fun for them, like a slumber party. She could hear it in their playful whispers.

That night, Lisa had a private talk with each of the family leaders. "Do you understand the rules? Do you know that our lives may depend on our total quiet and secrecy? I am trusting you to take charge of this room. Come to me the minute something, even the slightest thing, seems wrong. See that no one moves from their beds until I come by again in the morning."

And from the outside, Glenbard was still the deserted old high school building. There was positively no sign of life.

Although it was never known to the children, there *was* a light—a secret light—in one part of Glenbard. A small candle burned in a tower room that had been carefully sealed to prevent the smallest sliver of light from escaping. Wooden panels covered the window and the door to the hall. The edges were taped shut with black tape. It was like a sealed chamber—tight and lightless as a coffin.

The secret room was Glenbard's council chamber and it would glow inside for many, many nights to come. It was here, in endless meetings, that the future of the city would be shaped.

The candle's light shadow-painted the faces of the three leaders as they sat whispering around the small table.

Lisa was in charge of these conferences. Tonight they were discussing the ugly old problem of a defense plan. None of them liked to talk about it, but it had to be done. And the new plan had to be *brilliant*.

Looking at her notes, Lisa made her defense pro-

posal. "The way I see it, the first thing to do is seal this
place up so that no one could possibly get in. I'm talking about steel and bolts, not wood and nails. We
should put solid steel covers over the inside of every
door and window. I noticed that all the doors in the
gym and bathrooms are made of metal. We could use
them."

"Hey, I know, Lisa," said Craig. "In the auto shop
classroom, there's some welding equipment. My Uncle
Elliot was a welder. I don't think you need electricity to
work it. You just light the end of the torch and gas
comes from the tank. There are lots of tanks down
there." It didn't make sense to Lisa right away.

"What's the point, Craig?" she asked.

"Well, we could weld the metal doors to the steel
window frames. Nothing is stronger than welding!" he
explained.

"What's wrong with bars?" asked Jill. "It will be awfully dark in here if the windows are all covered over. I
wouldn't like that."

"It's not what we like that counts right now," Craig
said. "Anyway, with bars someone could throw fire-
bombs inside or spy on us."

"It sounds all right to me," said Lisa, and she thought
a moment. "But just think of the work it would take.
There must be a thousand windows in this place." And
she thought again . . . . "Why not just the first floor
for now? Then Jill can have her light up here. Our
other defenses, I think, will take care of the upper stories. We don't want any changes to be seen from the
outside till the very last minute. Craig, can you get it all
set up first—everything cut and fitted and ready to go
so we can put them all up the last night?"

"I think I can," he said.

"Well, you check it out and report to us tomorrow night!"

Their plans were very detailed. They tried to consider every possibility. "No chances . . . can't take any chances." Those words were like a theme song at every council meeting. The mistakes of Grandville were always mentioned. This time they wanted to be sure.

They spent hours and hours plotting the defense. On many nights they talked until daylight. It was an odd feeling for them to walk out of their dark chamber into the bright sunlight of the hall. They left the room filled with the evidence of their labor—candy wrappers, piles of notes and drawings, and empty pop cans covering the table.

The defense plan was taking shape; it was complex and brilliant. "Napoleon himself could learn from it," Craig boasted one night.

They would dig a secret tunnel entrance from the bushes and then through the hill on Lake Road. Charlie's dogs would be a main part of the plan. "You'd better give us a progress report soon. And keep the dogs away from here till they're trained. We can collect them at the airport, in a hangar maybe," said Lisa, thinking of the risk the barking dogs would create in the next week.

But the roof defense was the main part of the plan. There'd be a dozen sentries pacing the roof line at all times. Dressed in black, and wearing black masks, they'd each cover about two hundred feet. A small storage shed would be built near each sentry's station, and it would hold guns, ammunition, and one hundred Molotov cocktails.

The brick-wall rim of the flat roof was a perfect shield. It even had spaced slots in it for guns to rest on, just like a real castle. The rim was just high enough to protect the sentry. Only his head would show above it. The rim's top would be lined with bricks, glass fragments, and paper bags of sand. During an attack, the sentry could run on a board along the edge, showering the enemy with missiles.

The children devised a very dangerous weapon for serious attacks. They put drums of oil next to each sentry shed. These could be heated, and pails of the boiling oil could be poured over the rim of the roof onto any enemies brave enough to scale the walls.

At half-hour intervals during the night, each sentry would drop a stone to the ground from his station. If the dogs stirred or barked at the sound, they would know that all was well—that the four-legged sentries below were alert and ready.

All these plans made up just a small part of Glenbard's total defenses. When the Glenbard flag was raised and the city was ready, nothing could harm them. There would be no need for face-to-face fighting. The children could defend their home without having to resort to offensive moves; all they had to do was watch and drop things over the rim. All combat would be defensive.

They created their other plans with just as much detail. In the night, the citizens of Glenbard slipped silently from the fortress and went to all the hidden parts of Glen Ellyn, loading, looting, training, and even spying. They moved about in perfect, efficient silence.

After the first week, the old high school still seemed deserted. "Where are the children of Grand Avenue?" old friends and enemies wondered.

Things were changing mysteriously around the town and it was puzzling to the other children. "Hey, where did that big pile of sand go? It was in front of the lumber yard yesterday." Or, "Look! Someone's been in the library . . . see, the shelves are almost empty." Or, "I thought I heard someone outside the house last night and then I heard the dogs barking. It was scary. It sounded like a hundred dogs barking all at once."

The night council meetings continued. "We'll never have it ready on schedule," Lisa complained one night, in the second week of their work. "How's Charlie's dog training coming along?"

"Okay, I guess, but I haven't been able to work at it for four days," Charlie explained to Lisa. "When there's snow on the roads, we can't go out. Our tracks will lead every enemy right to our door."

"Good thinking," Lisa complimented him. "I'm sure glad you thought of that! No chances. We just can't make any dumb mistakes."

"Okay," she said, bringing the meeting to a new topic. "I want to talk about an idea that I had last night. There is safety in numbers and we haven't come close to filling this place up. We just rattle around. There's too much work to do and too few kids to do it. Besides, it would be much safer if people were living in all parts of the building."

"Get to the point, Lisa," said Craig. He was tired. It had been a long day.

"Okay," and she glared at him. "It's just that I haven't thought it through very well. But I think we should fill Glenbard with child-families. I want to rent parts of our fortress to other kids."

"Oh, oh, here she goes again," said Craig to Jill. "I can't take this. I'm going to bed."

"Stay where you are. It's important," Lisa ordered. Jill was silent.

"You see, we've got something special here. Safety— and many things that other kids don't have, like the library, the gym, and the supplies.

"After Glenbard is finished, we can go all around Glen Ellyn telling kids about the nice life they could have here. If they are willing to follow our rules, and do their share of the work, we could let them join us."

"Yes," said Jill thoughtfully, "I think you're right, Lisa. In fact, I'm sure you're right. Just think of how much easier things would be. Julie and Nancy would have help with the cooking. Those kids are really overworked, you know. All of us are. And, we'd have more friends, more new ideas . . . and fewer possible enemies," she laughed, "because they'd be in with us, instead of out there joining gangs."

"Sure, but that's the whole problem," Craig said, still in his bad mood. "When we start adding people, they'll bring new problems with them. How many spies will we have? How many arguments will we have about rules and things? Suppose some group of kids decides to take over? And don't forget, more people eat more food."

He was right about the spy danger, and Lisa knew it. But she defended her idea. "I've thought a lot about those problems and I'm sure we can solve them. First, we'll have a written list of rules for the new people, and they'll have to sign an agreement, like a citizenship contract."

"I think we should just take families we know about personally," said Jill. "That way we'd be safer. I can think of at least a dozen child-families I know of that we could trust, and so could every other kid.

"How many people do you think we should plan for, Lisa?"

"Well," she answered carefully, "I think we should start really small, just to see what problems come up. Let's say, for example, that we took in three families to start with—no more than a dozen new kids altogether.

That would give my plan a good test, and we could grow from there."

Craig seemed encouraged by the test idea. His harsh look faded.

Lisa went on. "I have been studying the floor plan of Glenbard, and it seems to me that we might eventually have a city of about eight hundred."

Craig got up and left the room. "Eight hundred," he muttered to himself. "Eight hundred!" He felt like swearing out loud.

"He's really mad, Lisa." Jill started after him.

"Wait, Jill. Let him go. I'll talk to him when he cools off a little. Something else is bothering him too, I can tell. He's been acting strangely. I hate to say it, but I don't think he likes it here. He's probably got the farm on his mind again!"

The two girls talked about Lisa's new idea in detail. It seemed to have almost endless possibilities. "As soon as the city is finished, we'll go out and talk to some families. We'll each find one. Three families will make a good test."

"Yes, but let's not talk about it to Craig much. We'll wait and let him get interested on his own. Maybe he'll see that it would mean more students for his school, and more teachers, too. And even more farmers, for that matter."

The two girls stared at the candle for some time, thinking about the new plan. Finally Jill spoke, changing the subject.

"Lisa, why do you keep calling it your city—saying that it's your property."

"Because it is! I thought I told everyone that on the very first day."

"But we've all helped to build it, haven't we?" argued Jill. "The kids are starting to call you selfish. They don't like it when you call it yours. They want to feel they own it too."

"Selfish? I guess I am. But, there's more to it than that. Don't forget, it was *my* discovery. The place was just sitting here empty, belonging to no one. I found it, planned it, filled it with *my* supplies, and now I run it.

"Nobody else seems to want my job, you know. Craig will probably wind up going off to *his* farm. And you'll leave too, someday, and start *your* hospital. That's ownership, isn't it? Will it be selfish for him to own his own farm? Will people call him selfish for selling the crops from *his* farm?

"Why should this be any different, Jill? At first, I didn't think it made any difference at all, but then I started to imagine what would happen to Glenbard if more than one person was in charge. If the city belonged to no one in particular, we'd form a group that would vote on things. And that would be bad."

"Bad? How so, Lisa? Voting is a good thing. It's fair if everybody has a chance to help decide important things. You sure have some strange ideas."

Lisa ignored the insult. "Do you think it would be fair for the group to decide that all the supplies I found were suddenly community property, and that I don't have the right to decide how they should be used? What would stop them from deciding to vote away my right to the cars I find, now that I've taught children how to drive?

"No, Jill. I know that you like to share things, but it just doesn't work out the way you'd like it to. In the first place, nothing would ever get done. With no one in charge, no one to make decisions, the group would argue all the time about whose property should be shared. And then everybody would be squabbling about how to divide things up, and they'd be too busy to accomplish anything.

"I do own this place and I don't force anyone to stay. I didn't force you or anyone else to come here. It's a free thing. I'm willing to take the worries and the responsibility, but I'll keep the control, thank you," she said a little angrily.

"Call me selfish all you like, but I don't want to *own* anybody. I don't want anyone to *own* me, and that's what a sharing group wants to do.

"Think about it, Jill. Let's say, for example, that you have a hospital someday. *You* find a building. *You* reclaim Central Dupage Hospital with *your* ideas, *your* decisions, and *your* work. Running things is work, you know, hard work! Then, imagine that the people you'd hired to work in the building decide to form a group so they can help you run it. And, just suppose that you get some wild ideas, some really big, exciting plans for the hospital, and they decide that you're nuts. And then they vote the hospital away from you. Even if the vote was ten against your one, would that make it fair?"

"But, Lisa, this is different. Cities are never owned by people. They're much too big and complicated for one person to run."

"Ah, but you're wrong there, Jill. My dad was telling me about new cities owned by individuals, and they worked out much better, because no one *owned* anyone else. In those new places, no group could decide about your life or vote things away from you. And you had to run a good city, or people would leave it. Those cities were just getting started at the time of the Plague. In fact, there was a whole country being built that way—I read about it in a magazine. The place was called Minerva, The Republic of Minerva."

Jill didn't feel like arguing. "Well, anyway," she said,

"I think you're in for trouble if you keep calling it *your* city."

Lisa considered her next words carefully. "Freedom is more important than sharing, Jill. This is my city. I plan to run it well and build it into something good. But I must be free to do it the way I think is best." And she thought some more. "And if you, or Craig, or anyone else doesn't like it, then you can use *your* freedom . . . and leave."

Jill wouldn't leave Glenbard—not for a long while, anyway. But she did leave Lisa alone in the tower chamber. She was angry, like Craig, though her thoughts about Lisa weren't as critical as his. "She sure is stubborn. I hope she doesn't regret it!"

Lisa's thoughts about herself were more harsh. "You're not being very smart, Lisa. You need their help and it's dumb to make them angry. I suppose I can talk more about *our* city if that will make them happy. But I must never lose control. If I'm ever to rebuild things, it's got to start with this city. To fill Glenbard with eight hundred people would be good for every one of us; it would make life safer and easier." But she also began to see her job more clearly. She would have to work hard to *earn* her goals. She'd have to offer something better to the children than they could find anywhere else. "Like in the kingdom of Real Fun," she thought, and she smiled.

Lisa didn't sleep that night, except for brief moments when her head rested on her arms in front of the candle.

"I'd better write a contract of some kind for Glenbard—right now—before this 'group' thing gets out of hand."

And what she wrote in the next hours was a constitution for a new city.

When she had finished, she looked at the candle and thought, "It wouldn't get an 'A' from Mrs. Moran." Old memories of school days and play flashed through her mind. It all seemed so very long ago. The images of her parents, and by now even the house on Grand Avenue, had become fuzzy. She tried to recall those things more clearly. But it was no use; they were distant and blurred.

The past no longer saddened Lisa. Things changed so quickly, and her life was getting to be more fun each day. There were many exciting new things to look forward to—new problems to solve, and new ways of earning! It was as the wise king had said: "Earning things is more than just something, it is everything."

Sunlight was in the hall, but she couldn't tell from the tower chamber. Her head rested for a last few moments before the new day . . . and some strands of her hair fell loosely over the page she had just written.

The Glenbard Constitution was about freedom. Each citizen was free to leave if he or she ever wanted to. But he had to leave free of debt. There was a provision for that. Everyone had to earn his place in the city by the means decided upon by both parties—Lisa and the citizen.

There would be no rule by the group. It was Lisa's property; she would consider advice and try to be fair, but she had the authority. Lisa would be the judge in disputes among the citizens, but she would call on her council for advice.

The last provision of the constitution was most important: "It is against the law of Glenbard to use force *offensively* against anyone for *any* purpose."

It was a very simple constitution, and though it was disliked by many of the pioneer citizens of Glenbard, each one signed it. After all, they knew of no better place than the city the girl had created.

On the night of January 16, the ghostly old school building came mysteriously to life. Lights filled the upstairs windows, and there was joyous shouting and excitement on the roof. The glow of a dozen torches dotted the roof line. Horns blared, and a hundred dogs barked as if to drown out the sounds above them. To the silent audience below, Glenbard looked like a castle.

If you had been one of the faces hidden in the woods nearby, the wind might have blown you the smell of popcorn. And you would have been amazed by what you heard and saw.

Cherry bombs burst as they fell from the rim of the roof. Rockets shot at the moon and then fell to the lake below.

The children on the rooftop said that this celebration was even better than the first holiday in Grandville. And it was better because there was so much more to celebrate. The blistered hands that clapped and touched other hands had shaped something new and special. The lights in the sky were a tribute to their days of careful work.

The other children, watching from dozens of dark places, had the answer to their mystery. They knew where Grand Avenue had gone. They knew about the barking dogs and the strange night happenings of the past weeks.

If those watching children had been able to stand in the cold throughout the night, they would have learned even more. The celebration lasted till dawn. The citizens of Glenbard sang a new song, and they shouted cheers and challenges that broke the silence of the icy night.

In the morning, at the exact moment of sunrise, an awkward bugler sounded a new call . . . and ever so slowly, a bright orange-and-yellow flag was raised above the new city.

─── TWELVE ───────────────────

The next year was a busy, happy time at Glenbard. Word of the new city spread quickly. Every day new child-families called from the street below to a rooftop sentry, "Can we join your city?" And a committee of three would emerge from a heavy door under the protection of the riflemen on the roof. The committee asked questions: "Who are you? Where did you live? Why did you leave? What gang did you join? Who was the leader? Why did you quit? How can you prove your friendship? Do you understand what is meant by our constitution? Do you agree to add your name to it? Did your family have a car? A house? Will you trade them for membership in our city?" All of these had to be answered.

Many were turned away—not for lack of room, but because no one in the city knew them or because someone in the city *did* know them and said they couldn't be trusted. The committee couldn't afford to take any chances. Craig was the most skeptical of the three. He asked hard, tricky questions like, "Do you know my good friend, Tom Logan?" The unlucky child who said "yes" was sent away. And the unwise child who lied because he thought that the words ". . . friend, Tom Logan" were the key to getting in also had to go away.

But many new families were signed into Glenbard,

and the face of the city changed. There were crowds of
new citizens—they brought new ideas and a new spirit.
By summer there were ninety citizens and experiments
in farming. By September, the classrooms had over
three hundred students. The population grew and grew.

On January 16th of the next year, almost four
hundred citizens jammed the rooftop for the evening
celebration, and they shouted challenges to the armies
who still threatened silently below. By the end of April,
nineteen months after the Plague, Glenbard's population was just over five hundred.

The girl who owned the city was thought by some to
be very odd. "How could a girl own a city? Why *should*
a girl own a city? People don't *own* things like cities.
Did you read that silly constitution of hers?"

The girl who owned the city was not liked by everyone. "What does she do for Glenbard? We hardly ever
see her." But they knew she was not idle. It was ru-
mored that she only slept every other night, that she still
worked in a dark tower chamber. "What a silly thing!
There's no need for that anymore."

During the day, however, Lisa did make her presence
felt, inspecting the kitchen, or giving orders to workers
who were making new rooms ready, or sending her
trucks to secret supply places, or settling arguments between citizens.

Most of the children admired her and liked her
strong way of doing things. She seemed always busy,
and though she did not smile or laugh very often, they
could tell by the way she moved about that she was
happy. "You'd be happy, too, if you owned a whole
city," some said. "Did you know that she was the rich-
est girl in the whole world? What? You say it's just a
rumor and you don't believe it?"

Lisa spent a great deal of time in the library, looking

for ideas and answers for her city. The many books confused her and she was, at first, discouraged. The words were too big and the authors disagreed about everything. What was a good thing to one was an evil thing to a dozen others. Who was right? A leader needs to know about good and bad. But how could she learn to make the right decisions if all the great thinkers of history couldn't agree on their advice to her?

Then one day she made a lucky discovery—a single book with words and ideas she could understand because they applied to her life. They made sense to her. She never spoke about the book to anyone; it was her private treasure. She kept it safe behind a panel in the tower chamber.

She was finding that it wasn't easy running a city—especially one growing as fast as hers, but the special book helped her. There were problems every minute of the day. "Lisa, we're out of fuel for the torches," Charlie might tell her. And she would answer, "Well, I'll have it added to the supply list. It will be here by tonight. How much do you need?"

There seemed to be problems with everything—something different every day. Not enough books. "Then go get them from the Lombard schools." There was a big fight in the west wing. "Bring the fighters to me." Room 110 wouldn't be ready by tomorrow, and the Wilson kids were getting tired of living in the gym. "Well, get somebody to work through the night. We promised to have it ready!"

At council meetings, the big problems were discussed. The leaders seemed always to be one step behind. But still it was exciting. They had great fun at their meetings, laughing at the funny things that happened each day. They teased each other but grew to be very close friends.

"You're not going to believe what Lisa did today," said the construction manager. "She gave us drawings for the family rooms in the south basement area and forgot to put any doors in three of the apartments.

"This place is all confusion. You know what it's like to build walls without nails? Not easy. But it's even harder without wood! When can we get some lumber, Lisa?"

There were lots of problems. But the council had plenty of help. The new children brought new skills to Glenbard. They were all so happy to be free of gangs and starvation. For many months the problems seemed challenging and exciting.

"Planning is the secret," Lisa said over and over again. "If we can anticipate problems before they happen, then we'll succeed." They had never run a city before and they learned most of their lessons the hard way. But they seemed to be making enough right decisions. Things were going quite well. Soon Glenbard would be at full population. "Not bad for a year's work!" Lisa boasted. And then she admitted what was also true. "A year of *very hard work*," she said, as she studied the tired faces of her assistants—Craig, Jill, Steve, Todd, Charlie, and the six new council members.

Glenbard's defense plan was the biggest success of all. There had been eight enemy attacks and none of them had lasted more than ten minutes. Boiling oil in a soldier's face had a way of making gang leaders choose other targets.

There had been attacks by seven different gangs. Six never tried a second time. But Tom Logan tried twice. The second attack was cleverly planned, but not cleverly enough to beat the rooftop soldiers. Tom's face was scarred by oil burns from the second raid, and Charlie wondered if his hatred would bring his army back again. Tom now had one hundred and fifty men.

Charlie was turning out to be a brilliant military leader, but he was worried about Logan. "Lisa," he said at one council meeting, "I think he's gonna be back. Tom's no dummy. We've got to watch out for him. For some reason he's determined to get us."

"Charlie, you worry too much," she said. And looking at Craig, she added, "You generals are all alike!"

They both looked at her, and Craig said, "But, Lisa, you don't worry enough!"

Later that night, when Lisa was alone in the tower chamber, she thought about what Craig had said. "Maybe he's right. We can't take any chances. Logan could have spies in here already. And even if Tom does give up on us, there are other gangs. . . . No, they're not gangs anymore. They're becoming real armies. It won't be long before they'll have thousands of soldiers. We've got to be prepared."

She'd discuss it with Charlie tomorrow. They would figure out some new plan. Maybe a walking army of their own was what they needed. After all, they had five hundred and ten people . . . or was it five hundred and eighteen now? "I can't even keep track. It's growing so fast." She smiled at her own confusion.

Her thoughts turned to her ever-changing self. "They wonder why I seem so strong—they think I'm something special because I run my own city. Don't they see that it's fun, and that any one of them could do it, too? All you have to do is look at the old world for clues. A hundred books have ideas about building cities."

Then, in a harsher tone, she said out loud, "You know the truth, don't you, Lisa. You're still a child just like the rest of them. You wonder sometimes, don't you, why you got yourself into all of this. You're scared to death sometimes, aren't you. And tired, too." She tried to think of tomorrow's problems. It didn't work.

"They wonder why you sit in this dark room. They call it your 'chamber.' " But she knew why. "I can't leave this room or change it in any way. So many things began here. It's so private, and I can think so well here."

Then thinking became too burdensome, and she decided to inspect the roof sentries. She went outside. The fresh air felt good. It cleared her mind.

"How does it look tonight, Jody?" She was glad she had remembered the sentry's name.

"Looks just fine, Lisa. But you'd better tell Charlie to do something about those dogs. I dropped my stone a few minutes ago and there was no barking at all. They must all be sleeping. Maybe we've been feeding them too much." When he turned again to look at her, she was gone.

"Here, Jody! Come here and look. The dogs *do* seem to be sleeping—but it's not right. You can't feed them *that* much food. There's something wrong! . . . Something *is* wrong!

"Sound the 'quiet' alarm and get the militia up here. Now!" she ordered. While he passed the word, she ran to the other end of the building. All the dogs were lying still.

"I'm going down to see what's the matter," she called to the nearest sentry. "Get some kids with rifles over here to cover me. Here, help me with the rope ladder. Todd, is that you?" She had forgotten that *he* had sentry duty this night.

On the way down she realized her mistake. If there was trouble, why in the world was she going down into it? But it was too late—she was on the ground.

She went to the nearest dog—its body was quite cold. She ran to the next. Dead. She knew they had been poisoned.

She started to run for the rope ladder, but her path was blocked by a boy with a hideous scar on his face.

"Let me by!" she ordered, but he was not from Glenbard, and he grabbed her.

She bit him until he screamed and two soldiers came to his rescue. They held her and she couldn't move.

"Let me go! Sentry!" she shouted to the roof. "Pull the ladder up, quickly!"

"Lisa," the boy with the scarred face said, "it won't help for you to fight. I've got two hundred men surrounding your lousy Glenbard. It was nice of you to drop in," he laughed. "Don't you recognize me with my new face? I'm Tom. Tom Logan. Your boiling oil trick won't work tonight, Lisa. Your city is not your city anymore. It's *ours* now. So relax. I don't want to hurt you." And for a moment he seemed almost kind.

But she didn't believe him. She fought him and, somehow, she broke free and ran. "Stop, Lisa, or we'll shoot! Stop, Lisa! We don't want to. . . ."

Those were the last words she heard. There was a deadly pain in her somewhere and she fell, silent, near the bushes.

"Who did that?" Logan shouted. "I told you not to shoot until I gave the order. See if she's all right!"

The child-soldier who studied her body came back to Tom with his report. "I think she's dead. There's blood all over her head and she isn't breathing."

Tom shuddered. In all his violent days, he had never killed anyone. He knew it was a mistake, but did that really change anything? "Why her?" he wondered for a moment, before regaining his composure.

"Don't shoot till I say so!" he shouted. (For Lisa, at least, the order had come too late.) Next, Tom shouted a bluff to the sentry above. "We've got her! We've got your leader! So don't throw any of your junk down here or we'll kill her. And I mean it! Open the big door—we're coming in!"

And the army of Chidester, Elm, and Lenox streets did just that. They took over Glenbard without resistance. They had the guns and the girl who owned the city.

"You see!" boasted Tom Logan to his captains. "I *knew* it would work. Wasn't I right?" And they all knew that *he* was the rightful leader of the city.

Tom's soldiers were everywhere. The citizens of Glenbard were frightened, helpless. Their lives had changed into a nightmare. What had happened to *her,* they wondered.

"Where is Lisa?" Craig demanded.

Tom bluffed again. "We're keeping her below in a safe place, just to be sure you don't do something stupid. You know we'll kill her if you try anything dumb!" He sounded tough.

"You're the next in command, aren't you, Mr. Green Thumbs?" Tom wanted to hurt Craig. "Well, you go right now and tell your citizens that the joint is under new ownership. Go ahead, now . . . tell them! And while you're at it, tell them not to try anything dumb. Remember, we've got Lisa!"

What could Craig do but turn Glenbard over to Logan? The girl who built the city was now suddenly powerless—a captive, or worse.

THREE

*Fear is what you feel when you wait
for something bad to happen . . . and fun
is what you have when you figure out
a way to make something good happen.*

─── THIRTEEN ───

The smallest sentry had been watching the encounter. When he saw the girl fall near the bushes, he dropped to the roof and began sobbing. No one loved the girl like that sentry. She was more than just a sister. She had been wise, and kind, and brave, and he was proud of her.

No one noticed the little boy on the roof. He lay there in the darkness, crying, while the others met Tom Logan.

But, after a time, his grief abated and he began to think. "Is she really dead?" he wondered. How could he know for sure? He had to find out for himself. "Lisa can't be dead," he decided, as he climbed down the rope ladder.

When he came near her, he was sure that it was true. And he fell upon her body in tears. "No! Not Lisa!" He couldn't believe that such a dreadful thing was possible. For a long time he rested his head on her chest.

He moved suddenly. "She's breathing. She . . . is . . . breathing! Lisa, *Lisa!*" He whispered it, fearing that some enemy would hear.

"She's okay. She's alive!" Then the smallest sentry sprang into action.

Todd realized that he had to get help somehow. He knew that the enemy was everywhere inside Glenbard.

And soon roof guards would be assigned. He climbed the wall and moved the rope ladder around the roof rim to a place directly above Craig's window. He lowered himself, slowly.

The window was locked, and Craig wasn't there. Erika was sleeping in her bed, and he knocked on the window. She turned and saw him hanging there. He put his finger to his lips. Cautiously, she came to open the window.

"What are you doing out there, Todd?"

"Don't you know what's happened?" he asked her. "They've shot Lisa and taken over our city. Haven't you heard?"

"Oh, no!" she cried. "I didn't know, Todd. Is Lisa hurt bad?"

"Yes, I think so. There's blood all over her, but she's still breathing." He didn't know if she was seriously hurt. "I can't come inside, Erika, so you'll have to help me. Can you pretend that you're sick . . . ah . . . with a stomachache?" She didn't understand. He continued: "Try to look real sick, and go find Jill. Get her to take you to the hospital room. Tell her your stomach hurts. And you must also find Craig. Have him come with you and Jill. Keep acting sick enough to make Tom Logan believe it, and he'll leave you alone in the hospital room. I'll be waiting outside the window with a ladder. We must take Lisa away, and I need help.

"Pretend like you want to throw up. Try it now! so I can see . . . good, that should work." She looked awful. "Be careful, Erika, and hurry. Please hurry."

The smallest sentry climbed back to the roof and walked the rim to a point above the nurse's room. But he wasn't sure which window it was. "Was it two windows over from the chamber tower, or was it three?"

He couldn't remember. "I'll have to take a chance," he thought, and climbed down.

"Where are they?" he wondered, looking into the spotless room. "Hurry, hurry!" . . . and then he thought about his sister. "We're coming, Lisa!"

"Hurry, hurry! Please hurry! What could have gone wrong?" he asked himself. Suddenly the door opened and four people entered the room. Todd jerked his head away from the glass. Tom Logan was with them. He seemed to stay for a long time, arguing with Craig.

Todd peeked in now and then at the edge of the window. "Boy, does Erika ever look awful. I'm afraid she'll actually throw up. . . . Good, he's leaving now." And he watched Tom Logan assign a guard to the hall and close the door behind him.

They opened the window and Jill whispered, "Where is she hurt? What shall I bring? The stretcher? Yes! Throw it down to the ground, Craig. Could she talk? Here, fill your pockets with bandages and get some alcohol . . . and . . . oh, what else will we need?

"That should be enough. Let's go quick. Erika, you'd better come with us." Todd was the last one down. He shut the window and for some reason, when he did, the latch fell into place, locking the window from the inside. "Figure that one out, Logan," Todd said to himself. When they reached the ground, they ran. Craig carried the stretcher.

"All the dogs are sleeping, Toddy!" Erika hollered.

"Shut up," Todd said, not caring that she had used his old nickname. He was glad the dogs were dead. They were quiet and maybe, because of it, Lisa could be saved. "Follow me." He led them to her body. "You help her, Jill. I'll get the car. Craig, you stand guard. Here's my gun. And, Erika," he added, "you keep your mouth shut." He was beginning to sound like this sister.

Lisa didn't move or even open her eyes as they slid the stretcher into the back seat. But she was alive. Too cool and silent maybe, but alive. "How is she, Jill? Can you fix her up?" Todd started the car.

"Where are we going to take her?" Craig asked.

When he heard the words "to the old farm on Swift Road," Craig was startled. "Finally, after all this time, she has brought me to the farm," he thought.

The beat-up old Cadillac carried the leaders away from Glenbard. The girl who owned a city was homeless.

The old farm proved to be a good place to bring Lisa. "Look, Jill," said Craig. "It has an oil heater with its own fuel tank. All we need is a match."

The warmth—something they had learned to do without at Glenbard—would help make the operating room comfortable. Jill ran all about, preparing the room and giving orders to Erika, Craig, and Todd.

Lisa rested unconscious, covered with blankets, on a sofa. She stirred once and mumbled something. "What did she say?" said Todd. Then she spoke again. "No chances, can't take any chan . . . ."

"I wish she hadn't laid on the ground for so long. She's lost a lot of blood," said Jill. They covered her with more blankets while Jill studied a first-aid book. She was very nervous about the task that lay ahead of her. At Glenbard, she had treated cuts and injuries of all kinds, but she didn't have the faintest idea about how to remove a bullet. "Nothing about it in this lousy book." She threw it down.

"Craig, tear this sheet into strips."

"How wide?" he asked.

"Oh, six inches will be okay. Todd, try to find some whiskey in the kitchen. Erika, bring me some clean sheets, all you can find. No! No! Look in the linen closet—over there."

She decided to use the big dining-room table for the operation. "Todd and Craig, you bring the small mattress from the back bedroom . . . *Good* . . . now go wash your hands."

"But, Jill, there's no water in this house," said Todd.

"Well, we've *got* to have water. Go find some quick. Get at least six full pails. Hurry! Go to the lake if you have to." Jill was getting panicky. Todd went out immediately. "Build a fire, Craig!"

Jill felt Lisa's forehead. "She's much cooler now than before. Where is that water? Did Todd actually drive to the lake? I should have suggested rainwater to him."

Todd finally came back and put two pails of water on the fire to boil. "Okay," said Jill. "Who wants to be my assistant?" The Bergman children hated the sight of blood. "Todd, will you help?" Yes, he said he would. "All right, scrub up. Wash like you've never washed before. We can't risk an infection. We can't take any chances." Then Jill was ready to begin. "Help me lift her up on the table."

Lisa looked very pale. In fact, so did Jill and Todd— but for different reasons. Jill undid the temporary bandage they had applied in the bushes. "She's still bleeding."

The sight of the wound would not have seemed shocking to nurses in a regular hospital. They might even have said that it was minor. But to the children, it was horrible. Jill faced an awesome responsibility. "Her life is in my hands. What if she dies? What do I do first?"

At the first sight of the blood, Craig and Erika left the room. "Todd, we've got to get that bullet out," Jill said. "Let's just do it!" And then her courage returned.

154   O. T. NELSON

"First, we've got to wash away the dried blood. Bring warm water and the strips of cloth." He returned. "Now tear the strips into small pieces the size of washcloths. Are you sure your hands are clean? Here, pour some of this alcohol in a pan. We can dip our hands in it, now and then."

With warm water and soap, Jill dabbed away the dried blood. When it was clean, the wound didn't look bad at all. Only a small hole in the arm, where the bullet was lodged. "She must have fallen on her head," said Jill. "See the big bruise and cut by her eye? That's why there was so much blood on her face."

Now Todd understood why the Chidester soldier had pronounced Lisa dead. When he had seen all the blood on her face, he must have thought that it was coming from a *bullet*. And that's why he had taken her for dead!

Jill soaked the area around the wound with alcohol and then began to feel nervous again. "So far it's been fairly easy, but how am I going to get the bullet out? Should I cut a wider opening? Suppose I hit an artery?"

She picked up the first-aid book and looked for the diagram of the circulatory system. She studied it over and over, looking from the page to Lisa's arm and back again.

"Oh, I get it now!" she shouted happily. "A small cut *this* way won't hurt anything, Todd. Hold the blade of the razor in the flame for thirty seconds. That will sterilize it." Lisa stirred, but nothing more. "It's a good thing she's still unconscious. I don't think she'd want to be here for my debut as a surgeon."

"Is she going to be all right?" Todd asked.

"Yes," Jill replied.

"Here goes." She was trembling and she wanted to close her eyes. She made a shallow, two-inch cut. The tiny bullet was lodged by the side of Lisa's arm bone, not far from the surface of the skin. Jill could feel it.

"Give me more pieces of cloth. No, better yet, Todd, you keep dabbing the blood away, and I'll try to get the bullet out. Dab two or three times with each piece, then soak one in alcohol and dab just once. Keep that up. Always use a fresh piece of cloth."

With a pair of tweezers, Jill reached into the opening and felt for the metal. "There it is," she said, and she carefully removed the bullet. Tears filled her eyes.

"Todd, I'm closing the wound . . . get more alcohol . . . then we'll stitch it up. That won't be easy, but I think I know how."

"That wasn't too bad, was it?" she said, when they'd finished. "I think I'll make a good doctor someday." Todd thought she would too.

In the middle of the night, Lisa woke up. Todd was sitting by her side. "Hi, Lisa," was all he said. She nodded to him. He could tell, as the drowsiness left her, that her arm hurt a lot. She groaned and turned away.

"Jill, come here!" Todd called. And when she came into the room, he whispered, "I think something's wrong."

"Arm hurt?" asked Jill, not seeming very concerned. Lisa nodded again. "That's to be expected. We fixed you up just fine, but we had to do a little . . . ." She started to tell the story of the surgery, but, fearing that she would alarm Lisa, she said instead, "We had to do a little work on your arm. It will feel better soon."

"I know just what you need," Jill said, returning from the kitchen. She handed Lisa a glass of golden-colored liquid. "Now, drink it all, even if you don't like the taste."

The drink looked much better than it tasted. Lisa took a big swallow and spit it out over the blanket.

"Now, Lisa," Jill teased. "Have you forgotten your manners?"

"Ick!" Lisa made a horrible face. "What was that stuff?"

"Whiskey," Jill answered, as if it were an everyday children's drink.

"Are you trying to get me drunk? What kind of friend are you?" In spite of her pain, Lisa was teasing too. Friendship and this kind of sharing were better than whiskey.

"I'm serious, Lisa. Drink it all up. You'll need it for the pain, and you have to get some more rest." Jill handed her a full glass.

It took a long time for Lisa to finish it. But, strangely, it got easier for her as the glass emptied. The last swallow was a big one. Lisa giggled. "Boy, do I feel funny."

Then Jill told Lisa about what had happened that day. "Well," Lisa said, "sometimes one mistake is all it takes. I suppose, in a way, if I could make a stupid error like that, I deserved to lose the city. You've got to be smart to earn good things.

"And even that's not enough. You've got to be smart to keep them, too. . . ." After a long pause, she said, "I guess I'll just have to earn it all back. I'll figure something out."

Then the whiskey glow changed Lisa from a wounded leader into a dizzy schoolgirl. She started giggling.

"I give up," Jill said. "You're drunk. Get some sleep. Call me if you need anything."

"That's okay," said Todd. "I'll be here to help her."

And that night it was Todd who was the storyteller. He started with a serious tale about a little prince in a faraway kingdom. But Lisa giggled in all the serious places. So he tried to change it into a funny, silly story. But he couldn't finish it either—just couldn't concentrate. Soon, Lisa fell asleep.

Todd wasn't bothered by his failure as a storyteller. He knew his audience was at fault. He turned out the light and sank into the big chair. It was not comfortable. He decided to sleep on the operating table.

As he fell asleep, Todd thought about his sister. He was glad that she was better. And he was learning so much from her. "Does she know that?" he wondered.

He thought of the funny change the whiskey had made in her. She woke up in pain and fell asleep giggling. "Maybe," he thought, "she should get shot more often!" He would tell her his joke in the morning.

The light in the Glenbard tower chamber burned through the night. A scarred face stared into the candle. "Who shot her?" he wondered. "I'll beat his little head in if I ever catch him."

Tom Logan was mad. But *not* because he thought Lisa's death would make the citizens of Glenbard hate him, or because this hate would make his job of leadership harder. No, Tom Logan was mad because he hadn't wanted Lisa to be hurt. At least not that way. He shook when he recalled, again, that he'd killed her. He was mad, too, for his luck, because that's all the victory really was. And he was mad, most of all, at his own nameless fears.

——— FOURTEEN ———

The new leader of seven hundred sat before the dawn, still thinking—and planning how to manage his first day in the city. He stared into the black void of the chamber, past the candle that had burned away. "The candle," he thought. "It was her candle and now the light is gone . . . and she is gone."

The new leader of only four lay awake before the dawn, thinking and planning how to bring back all that had been lost. She stared into the ever-brightening space of the window until the sunlight poured in. Her body felt weak, but her mind was active. "The city," she thought. "It was my city and now I am gone from it. I *must* go back!"

When the warm room was filled with sunlight, Todd opened his eyes. He stared at the strange ceiling until he recognized the lamp hanging down above him. He remembered that fixture as the one that had hung ominously over the operating table. Why had he slept there? Then he remembered the events of the night before and, in a quick motion, he turned his head to study the patient.

Her eyes were open, and they met his. She had been staring in his direction for some time. She said, "It's nice to wake up warm in the morning, isn't it, Todd? Maybe we can find more oil stoves and move them to Glenbard. Think of how cold it must be in the children's bedrooms. We should . . . ." The reality of what had happened came back to her and she fell silent.

Then, Lisa and Todd each tried to construct a mental image of the distant city. What was it like now? Would they ever see it again? Of course! They both knew they would.

Todd was in a good mood. It was fun being in the cheerful farmhouse, and he remembered the joke he had wanted to tell Lisa the night before. "You sure were acting silly last night, Lisa. You should get shot more often!"

She smiled and said, "Thank you for saving my life, Todd!"

"How do you feel, Lisa?"

"My arm hurts quite a bit. Do you think you can find some aspirin for me, Todd?" He slipped from the table and started rummaging through the nursing supplies.

Jill appeared at the doorway. "What you need is a glass of whiskey, Lisa."

"Are you kidding? That stuff is awful—not a chance." Lisa made a face. "I can still taste it from last night." She shook her head. "I'd rather suffer. Can't I have some aspirin?"

"Sorry, Lisa, but we forgot to bring it along," Jill said. "And this farm doesn't have any. In fact, the whole place is empty. Someone has been here already. Suit yourself, Lisa. There's plenty of whiskey.

"Come on, Todd. Get your coat. We'll go find some supplies. I'm starved. Maybe there will be something at the farmhouse across the road."

Jill and Todd left, and the cheerful room was silent. Lisa remembered suddenly that it was *she* who had been to this farm and emptied it. She had been the one, a long time ago, who had taken the food and even the aspirin. Now she remembered. The old woman's note, her wild idea about driving the car, her first exciting ride, the chicken in the wicker basket, and the cookies in the jar. Yes, it seemed a long time ago. So much had happened in the months since.

At first, Lisa's plans were without form. She had left an urgent need to recapture Glenbard since she first awakened. And now that need and her excitement made her forget the pain in her arm. Aspirin or whiskey couldn't have done the job as well.

Lisa knew that they could save the city. She didn't doubt it for a moment. But winning it back would take much more than her confidence. How could four win a battle against an army of hundreds? She, better than anyone, knew the strength of the fortress. "How? . . . How? . . ." she asked a hundred times. And then the first seed of a plan began to grow in her mind. Soon ideas were streaming through her consciousness. Lisa didn't notice as the others came in the door.

"Of course," she said out loud. "It will cost me plenty, but I can make a deal with another army. For two months' worth of supplies, they'd help me capture the city. The dogs are gone . . . that will help. And we know the city better than Logan. . . . I wonder if anyone told him about the secret tunnel? If only we could get a spy inside."

She laughed to herself at the thought. "A spy? Why we have five hundred spies in there, or was it five hundred and ten?" She laughed again, and the breakfast-makers turned to look at her. Was she delirious?

Far from it. Her thinking had never been clearer. The ideas kept coming. Signals from a spy . . . a new

plan of the city showing Logan's room . . . a hired
army surrounding the city . . . disguises for the four of
them . . . a daylight attack on the inside from the tunnel . . . a signal to the army on the outside. . . .

"Lisa, do you want some breakfast?" a voice asked.

But she didn't hear. "Could we get to Logan without
being detected? It should be a dawn attack. He's probably a late sleeper. A set of keys. We'll need that to get
into his room. A small pistol. . . ."

"Her eyes are wide open, and her lips are moving a
little," someone said.

"That's it," she thought. "A gun to his stupid head.
We'll hold him hostage till his army is out of the building, and then we'll lock him up for safekeeping. If we
threaten to kill him, they'll leave us alone, at least till
we can get our defenses back. Suppose the army doesn't
need Logan anymore and they decide to fight instead of
walking out. They've probably gotten to like it in there.
I'll bet they've eaten up all the treats. What if they fight
us? Will they believe our threats about killing Logan?
We have to take the chance. We'll signal our soldiers,
and they'll slip in through the tunnel too. You can't see
the entrance from the roof. Then when Chidester is
gone, we can get back to work. . . ."

"Should I shake her, Jill?" Todd asked.

The battle was already fought and won in Lisa's
mind. "When they're gone, we'll have to figure out a
different kind of 'moat'—one that's safer than a ring of
dogs. And we should find more cars with gas, or find a
way to get more gas. The parking lot is filling up with
empty cars. What had Ron Kerwood said about porta-
ble electric generators? They run on gas, too, and we
could get electricity from them. . . . Just think of that!
We'd have lights and stoves and refrigerators . . . and
music. . . ."

She turned suddenly toward the breakfast table. "Music!" she shouted. "Music! Do you kids know that we haven't heard music in almost nineteen months?"

They stared at her. The loud words startled them.

"Music, I said. Soon we'll have music at Glenbard." She couldn't understand their dumbfounded looks.

Now they were sure she was delirious. Jill walked over to the couch and stroked Lisa's forehead. "Relax awhile, Lisa," she said. "Relax. We have food whenever you're hungry. Do you want a glass of water?"

Then Lisa understood. "Thanks, Jill. Really, I'm all right. I was just thinking about a plan to get the city back, and I guess I got carried away."

"Do you think you can walk to the table?" Jill asked. "We've made a nice breakfast. Yours may be a little cold by now, though."

Lisa tried to stand but fell back to the couch. Jill said, "You're weak, you know—you lost a lot of blood. Stay on the couch. I'll bring your food to you." The other children gathered by the couch to watch her eat.

"Eggs? Juice?" Lisa was amazed. "Where did you find this stuff?"

While she ate the delicious cold egg, Todd explained. "The farm across the road has a big supply of everything. There was a jar of Tang in the pantry, and we found a chicken under the blankets in a bedroom. We couldn't figure out what she ate but she had a nice bed and a nice house all to herself. That's how we found the egg for you."

"Smart chicken," Lisa said, with a smile. "I'll have to go meet our new neighbor and thank her for the breakfast. We must be neighborly and all that, you know!"

Craig continued the game. "I wonder if the old bird is afraid of chicken gangs?"

They each tried a joke about the chicken, and though

the jokes got poorer and poorer, they laughed harder
and harder. Everyone was feeling quite giddy and silly.

Finally, Jill stopped the fun with a serious question.
"Lisa, what did you mean when you shouted the word
'music'? And why did you say we'd soon have music at
Glenbard?"

Lisa told them about the electric generator and a little about the new strategy, but not all. She had to think
it through more carefully. And she found herself suddenly tired again. But she thought there were a few
things that they could get started on.

"Jill, can you figure out a perfect disguise for Todd?
He's going to have to be our spy. It must be a perfect
disguise, though. I'd hate to think of what they'd do to
him if he was ever caught." Jill nodded and thought
about it.

"Todd, will you do it?" Lisa asked. "You can slip in
and out during the night and spend your days as a
Glenbard citizen. You'll have to tell us how the place is
set up now. And you can pass messages to our friends
inside."

"Sure, Lisa," he said.

"Okay, then get to work on the disguise. Todd
should leave tonight. I'm tired now, and I feel like resting a little while. Let me know when the disguise is
ready."

Lisa wanted to think more about the plan, but the
sun was warm on her body and soon she was fast
asleep. She was still very weak. The whole day passed
while she lay on the couch. Her plans drifted in and out
of her dreams. Sometimes she was in a battle. At other
times, she was in her chamber plotting a bright new future. She had no nightmares.

Jill and Todd tried many disguises. Most of them
were hilarious. But none of them seemed to be "real"

enough. They tried marking his face up with fake scars
and parting his long hair down the middle. They dyed
his hair according to the directions on a package that
they found across the road at the "chicken's" farm.
They laughed at the dark-haired Todd. But the disguise
still wasn't good enough. "What can we do?" they wondered.

In the meantime, Craig spent most of his day out in
the sun with Erika. They saw the horror of the cattle
barn. They saw the wonderful modern equipment in the
huge garage—a new tractor, a corn picker, a set of
plows. "With all this stuff, I guess it's a big farm," said
Craig. "Eighty acres anyway." But he couldn't be sure
from the farmyard.

While Erika played in the empty chicken coop, Craig
went inside to investigate the old farmer's study. He
touched every book and thumbed through many of
them. "This man knew what he was doing," Craig concluded. "Just look at all his records. It'd be a cinch to
get it going again!"

He searched through all the drawers of the desk until
he found what he wanted—a big ring of keys. He
picked them up and ran out of the study. He stopped
when he saw Lisa's sleeping figure. For some reason, he
tiptoed past her and slipped out the door, shutting it
soundlessly behind him. Then he ran at full speed to the
equipment garage. Was he afraid to let her know what
he was thinking? He would tell her his decision later.

Now all he could think of was the tractor. "Come on,
Erika!" he ordered. "Hop up on the seat with me. Sure
there's room. We'll make room. We're going to take a
tour of our new farm. Yes, we're going to live here. It's
almost spring. No, it *is* spring! It's the middle of May—
don't you feel it today? Pretty soon we'll be planting our
crops. You're a big girl now, Erika. Do you think you

can run the house and learn to cook? . . . Sure you can! If I can learn to farm, you can learn to cook!"

While they talked, Craig fumbled with the gear shift on the tractor. He pushed and tugged and wished he could swear. Maybe that wasn't the shift lever, and he tried every other stick or button he could reach. No . . . nothing. Finally, he gave up and said, "I'll figure it out later. Come on, Erika, we'll just have to walk around our farm."

The walk took several hours. It was a much larger farm than he'd imagined. And by the time the tired children came back to the farmhouse, they had seen every inch of fence on the place and knew that they would like their new home.

Erika laughed at what she saw inside. So did Craig. The laughter pulled Lisa from her long dream. She turned her head toward the happy sounds and blinked her eyes in disbelief.

"Who are you?" asked Lisa of the visitor. "Where did you come from? Do you live on a farm nearby?"

The visitor grinned in a way that made Lisa mad. "Who are you?" she repeated, and now it sounded like a command more than a question. The others laughed and Lisa turned her head away in frustration. "Okay, don't tell me. I'm going back to sleep."

The little girl with the black hair was wearing a print dress. She said in a voice that Lisa recognized, "Don't you know me?" Lisa turned her head back to look again. She squinted through the candlelight for a closer look.

Then she laughed. "Todd!" was all she said. The disguise was good. She never did ask Jill how she'd managed to get him to dress like a girl, and she resisted the urge to tease her brave little brother.

After dinner Lisa briefed Todd for his mission.

"Take the car. Park it in Jill's old garage. Slip into Glenbard through the tunnel and wait in the furnace room until you can hear noises upstairs. That will mean it's daytime. Then be ever so careful and sneak into the south basement section of apartments. Make sure that there are crowds of kids in the hallway before you walk around. Look for the Johansen family's room—they're the newest and no one will notice if there are five Johansens instead of four. You will be Sheri Johansen. Explain to them only—no one else. Tell them who you are and that their lives depend on keeping your secret. Stay with them all day until you're sure you can trust them."

Lisa stopped to think a moment and then continued. "During the day, you must find out two things. First, where is Logan's room? And second, what kind of defenses do they have? There's one other important thing, Todd. If it's safe . . . *if it's safe,* try to see Charlie and tell him that we're okay and that we plan to take over on May 26th—that's six days from today. And tell him that we need at least ten cars, three large trucks, drivers to go with them, and all the guns he can sneak out. Tell Charlie that he mustn't talk to anyone or do anything about the plan for two days. He must first make his own careful plan for getting the men, trucks, and guns. When he's sure it will work, he can go into *silent* action. He and his team must sneak out of Glenbard on the night of May 23rd and come to the Arco station at Swift Road and North Avenue. We'll meet them there at midnight. Tell Charlie that if it's safe for us to show ourselves, he should flash a light across North Avenue every minute for twelve minutes, starting at midnight. Set your watch and give it to him. Then tomorrow night, after everyone is asleep, you slip out of the Johansen's room, down the hall, and out the tunnel. But please be careful—they may have guards. Here's a pistol—keep it under your dress. Use it if you have to . . . will you?"

"It's much too complicated for him," she thought. So she explained it all over and over and over again, until he could repeat the mission plan without error.

"I've got it now, Lisa," he said, finally, and he went out the door and disappeared into the night.

They all worried about him. It was a dangerous mission. But he was a brave boy. Finally, all but Lisa fell asleep.

"He can do it. I know he can do it," she thought.

The next day was a nervous day for all of them. "How is Todd? . . . How is he doing?" They all wondered.

Craig spent most of his time outside in the warm May sunlight. "Why is he out there all the time?" Lisa wondered.

Her strength was slowly returning. Jill told her she'd have to rest in bed for at least a few more days. Lisa didn't like that. She knew she had many things to prepare for the 23rd. But she contented herself for the rest of the day with making plans.

Late on the first day of Todd's mission, Lisa called for Craig, "What's the matter with you?" she asked. "You're outside all the time. Don't you want to help me plan the recapture of our city?"

"That's funny, Lisa," he said. "It was *your* city. Your very *own* city when you owned it. Now that we have to fight to get it back, it's suddenly become *our* city."

He was right and she knew it. Still, he hadn't answered her question. "I'm sorry," she said. "Will you help me plan the recapture of *my* city in which *your*

safety will be protected? . . . Craig, I didn't mean that
the way it sounded. I *need* your help now, I truly do. I
can't force you, I know that, and I would never want to.
But will you help me?"

"No," he said flatly. "Lisa, I think you should give it
up and stay here with Erika and me on this farm. Why
keep fighting?"

"Give it up? . . . Stay on this farm? . . . Craig, do
you think I'm crazy? What's on this farm but a tractor
and a lot of dirt?"

"But, Lisa, we're safe here, and we can live a peace-
ful life. We don't have to fight anyone. We can raise
our own food and let all the gangs kill each other off.
I'm tired of militias, and armies, and spy missions.
We're staying here!"

"You think you're safe here? Sure you are! Just
about the time you've hauled in your first crops, the
army of Chidester, Elm, and Lenox will stroll right in to
reap *your* harvest. What will you eat when they've
taken it all away from you? Who will defend you? Erika
with a pistol? Don't be dumb, Craig!"

"Don't *you* be dumb!" Craig challenged her. "Remember back on Grand Avenue when you said that the
militia would end all our problems? You said that same
thing again at Glenbard and look what's happened.
What you do, Lisa, is build valuable things that everybody wants to take away from you. So far they've done
it every time. Let them have it, Lisa. You can't fight
them forever. You'll work hard to build Glenbard into
an even richer and stronger fortress, and what you'll get
for your pains will be another attacking army—a bigger
and smarter one. Why fight it? Stay here with us, where
nobody will care about our life and our corn. At least
we'll be able to live in peace. No, Lisa," he concluded,
"we're staying here. I've decided that for sure!"

"I'm sorry, Craig. I'm sorry to lose your help and your brains to *this* place. Sure, I've made mistakes . . . I don't deny that. Sure, I've had wild ideas, and many of them have failed. Right now I'm the biggest failure in the whole world. But that's not going to stop me. I *know* I'm right. I *know* we can accomplish all those things I used to talk about. We can get everything to work again, someday. But, to do it, we've got to realize that the reason for all the fighting is fear! What do you think makes Tom Logan do what he does? It's fear. What do you think is the mistake almost everybody makes? They're afraid of the problem of survival. They fight and do all kinds of stupid things because they're afraid. No, I'm not giving up. It's too important. And I don't think that the rest of you are so afraid that you can't, someday, see it too." She was finished, and she turned away from her friend in resignation.

——— FIFTEEN ———

"Well," Lisa thought. "I'll just have to do it alone. But why doesn't anyone else see how simple it is? And how much fun?"

Jill had been listening to their argument and, although Lisa couldn't be sure, she guessed that Jill had taken her side.

"Jill," she said, "I think you should go back to Glenbard tomorrow. Katy and Missy must be really afraid without you. You can help Charlie with the planning . . . very secretly, of course."

And then she told Jill about her plans. Jill could help with signals to Lisa on the day of the attack.

"Tom will wonder why you've suddenly come back to the city. Tell him that I was only wounded that night and that you tried to save my life, but I died. Tell him we talked and I didn't blame him for the shooting. I knew it was just an accident. And tell him you want to live there under his leadership, to be with Katy and Missy and to run the hospital. I think he'll believe you and let you stay."

It must have been two o'clock in the morning when Todd returned to the farmhouse. He was very excited as he told them the news.

Tom Logan was having trouble running the city. He couldn't convince the citizens that Lisa was safe as his hostage. Most of the children thought she was dead. There were many rumors. They blamed Tom for her death and were doing everything they could to make his life miserable. He sat up late at night in the lonely chamber trying to figure out what to do next.

"Ah," Lisa thought. "He's learning what it's like to run a city and sit alone in that chamber. But it must be hundreds of times harder for him. The citizens are against him."

Todd went on. "He treats the children cruelly. He beats the ones who give him trouble. But no one has asked, yet, about any secret entrances to the city. He beat Charlie last night trying to get him to tell about the Secret Places, but Charlie wouldn't tell, Lisa! He wouldn't tell—no matter what Logan did!"

"Good for Charlie," Lisa said. "There's at least one other person who's not afraid. Good work, Todd! I know you haven't had any sleep, but can you slip back in tonight?"

"I'm not tired, Lisa. What do you want me to do?"

"Good fellow," she said, and then thought, "there's another citizen who isn't afraid."

"Okay, here's what you do next. Go back to the Johansen's room, sleep there, and wake up tomorrow with them. Tell Charlie that Jill will be coming in during the day and not to believe what she says. She'll tell them I'm dead. We hope Tom will be less suspicious once he learns that and won't notice our work on the 23rd. Then ask Charlie to explain his plan to you so we know what's going on before we meet him at midnight."

Todd understood perfectly. He was becoming a good spy. In the darkness, he set off on his new mission. For the next forty-eight hours he would have no sleep.

Lisa was still confined to the couch, but she felt much better. Her mind, too, was finding new strength—

gaining new confidence. Her defeat had made her think more clearly. She knew, at last, the meaning of the word "logical." And the old warning, "take no chances," was a constant sentry in her mind. She began to think of each problem that confronted her as a new opportunity—a challenge. Defeat had taught her a lesson and strengthened her mind. And what improved her mind, of course, improved her life. Each challenge was exciting—something new to figure out.

"Take no chances . . . take no chances . . . look at all the possibilities . . . mistakes are costly . . . be logical . . . keep your mind clear . . . think . . . think . . . plan . . . be logical . . . take no chances!"

The words ran through her mind, over and over again, as she plotted the new strategy. Lisa had learned the price of carelessness, and with that knowledge came a new clarity of mind.

"The Great King was right," she suddenly realized. "When he said that the real fun in life is earning values, he was talking about the *most* important things in life—like knowledge, and love, and happiness—not just the things you can touch, like money and cars and stuff.

"Just look at me," she said to herself. "I've lost my city and all its treasures, but it hasn't crushed me. Only my body was hurt. And the city was only the symbol of what I've earned. My mind is clear. My friends are still friends. And my dreams, my plans, are not impossible. They become more real each day.

"What *have* I lost, really?" she asked herself. "I've made a mistake, and I'll never make it again. I've learned so much. I'm stronger than ever now. And when I get the city back . . . if I *earn* the city back . . . then I will be better able to keep it."

She stopped suddenly, feeling self-conscious. "What have I been saying?" Even she couldn't believe that she had found a truth. "I'm not quite twelve years old. It must be a dream." She shook herself, but she couldn't escape the truth. Words . . . words . . . some were hers, some were the king's, and some were her father's. A part of her ecstasy had its roots in the quiet nights in the chamber, while she pondered the special book. And part of it sprang from the fantastic history of the last nineteen months.

She had plans to make and so very little time. "I should stop playing with ideas and get to work. Why am I thinking about earning again?" And why did that word bring back a vision from the old world?

In her memory, the girl was six years old and sitting before a meal with her family. The father and mother argued about saying prayers at mealtime. One of them said, "We must be thankful to God for all we have."

The other asked, "Why? We should be thankful to our natures that we can earn our food and be thankful to ourselves that we have done so."

Were God and "natures" the same thing? The little girl wasn't sure. But from that day on the family had a new table prayer . . . no, it wasn't really a prayer at all . . . the family did not fold their hands or bow their heads. They would look calmly and purposefully at each other and say:

As we have earned this food, so must we earn all that is valuable in our lives.

Then, somewhat regretfully, Lisa turned to the day's reality once again. "Recapturing the city won't be easy. . . ." But she was ready for whatever might happen. "Another problem to solve," she thought. Lisa reviewed the list of problems that she had faced since the

Plague. Some of them had led to defeat, but many had ended in victory. For nineteen months, she had been in constant motion—finding supplies, planning militias . . . and she didn't have the time to notice that a windy day in May would have been good for kite flying. . . .

SIXTEEN

May 23rd was a warm evening. Lisa and Todd sat on their jackets and watched Swift Road for a sign of life. The Arco station was deserted except for the dancing reflections of moon and clouds in the faces of the gas pumps.

"What time is it, Todd?"

"Five minutes to twelve," he answered.

She said nothing more until a distant rumbling was heard. "What's that? Do you think it could be them?" They peered intently into the darkness.

Finally, the sounds took form. A convertible with its top down led the procession. Three soldiers accompanied a boy in the front seat. "That must be Charlie," Lisa thought. The convertible was followed by a large dump truck with twenty soldiers in the back. Three panel trucks and two cars were next. Each was filled with child-soldiers. At the end was another convertible filled with four more soldiers and a driver.

The string of vehicles stopped where Swift Road met North Avenue and, for a few minutes, everything was dark and silent. "What's the matter? Why isn't Charlie signaling?" Todd asked Lisa's unuttered questions.

And then a light flashed from the lead car. Todd and Lisa counted the seconds. ". . . Ten . . . thirty . . . sixty." Another flash of light. And then another. . . .

When the signal had been repeated twelve times, Lisa and Todd walked across North Avenue and approached the first car "Charlie, it's good to see you." She shook his hand and was in command again. "Gather all your men around the panel truck in the middle. Quickly! And tell them to be quiet."

None of the soldiers, not even Charlie, knew what was planned for that night. They all wanted to cheer when they heard the voice above them on the roof of the panel truck.

"We have a long wait ahead. At daylight, we will start an exciting tour. It will be our first trip away from Glen Ellyn. We will visit other cities in search of an army. When we find one that we think we can trust, then we'll make a deal with them to help us recapture Glenbard.

"We will go to Lombard first, then to Villa Park, and then back to Wheaton. If we can't find what we want, we'll try other cities. But. . .

"You there," she said impatiently to a restless soldier. "Did you hear what I said?" He did not answer. "You must all pay total attention to what I say. We can't take any chances tomorrow. Who knows what we'll find in those other towns. Maybe there'll be armies that could kill us on the spot. We must be ready! We can't make any mistakes. So pay close attention."

And they began to rehearse their strategy. The soldiers rested for a time, while Lisa and Charlie sat by the Arco pumps discussing the weaker aspects of their plan. When they agreed upon a way to strengthen the mission, they would rouse the soldiers for more briefings. Lisa carried the plan beyond the events of the next day. Her strategy brought them to the morning of May 26th when Charlie's soldiers and a hired army of hundreds would recapture the city.

"Lisa, why get ahead of ourselves? Let's take the plan one day at a time." The general criticized her.

"No, Charlie. We must plan the whole strategy to make sure that everything fits together. Then we can adjust it each day, as we need to, until the 26th."

They spent the entire night in conferences and briefings. The soldiers slept and were awakened and then slept again. By morning the plan was fixed in everyone's mind.

The eight vehicles and the army of fifty-five made ready just before morning.

At dawn, the motorcade began the journey to Lombard. The children were tired; some were frightened thinking about what they might discover in the "outside" world. But they were brave and kept to their assigned positions in the vehicles.

The people in the towns were amazed by the long motorcade. They ran into their houses—afraid that the brigade had come to do them harm. No one in these cities had yet learned to drive. The sight of one moving automobile would have shocked them, but to see eight cars and trucks filled with armed soldiers made them shudder.

The motorcade stopped many times in Lombard. Lisa and Charlie tried to learn who the town leaders were. A few of the less fearful children stayed outside to watch the procession, and when Charlie would call out, "We've come in peace, who is your leader?" someone would walk to the lead car. Then Charlie would say, "We are from Glen Ellyn. We want to be your friends. We are here in peace. Where is your headquarters?"

They stopped at least twenty times, but no one would tell about "leaders" or "headquarters." Lisa and Charlie decided that those words were no longer spoken there.

The appearance of the town itself seemed to confirm this—it was lifeless and dirty.

The motorcade moved on to Villa Park. What they saw there was something that no one wanted to speak of. It was a town that hadn't survived. Death was everywhere. The children felt its presence on every street of the town, and they didn't need to look inside a single door to know it was there. They drove away silently.

In Wheaton they found a leader, a headquarters, *and* an army—but not the alliance they were looking for. The general of Wheaton was a cruel, violent boy. "Get your army out of here," he said. "Or my men will wipe you out. I have two hundred soldiers. My name is Scott Donald Mennie."

"Scott Donald Mennie?" a voice called from the ranks. "Looks more to me like Scott Donald Duck!" The small army of Glenbard laughed, and Lisa studied the angry general. He was shaking, slightly.

He chose to ignore their insult. "You'll be smart if you just stay in your own town and don't stick your necks out of it again—ever!" And he told them why. "I'm going to join with the Chicago army and we'll be seeing you someday soon. So don't get too snoopy—or you'll just give us a reason to wipe you out early."

Then he bragged. "The Chicago army is an enormous and powerful force. It has over two thousand soldiers. And when Wheaton and other towns join up, it'll have even more. Maybe as many as five thousand by July. When we're ready, we'll start to capture towns, like yours, one at a time, until we control the whole state."

"He talks too much," Lisa thought.

But he wasn't finished yet. "If you're smart, you'll join us. If you're not smart, you'll regret it. The King of Chicago is very, very powerful. He'll see you soon, I'm sure. You'll have a choice. Take advantage of it.

"Now get out of here! But wait. What is your leader's name? Is he here? I want to give his name to the King."

When Lisa stepped forward, the boy laughed. "It's not true!" He laughed again, and this time he looked at the fifty-five soldiers. "A girl?" he mocked. "What's the matter with you guys? Boy, you must be some tough army with a girl leading you!"

And the girl who had never wanted to hurt anyone—ever—even Tom Logan, smashed her fist into the face of the Wheaton general.

The blood from his nose confused him long enough for the motorcade to pull away. "A girl!" he thought, as he stared after them in amazement.

"Well," said Charlie to Lisa. "We've got another enemy now . . . Scott Donald *Duck!*" And they roared with laughter at his distant figure . . . . Suddenly serious again, Charlie added, "That Chicago army stuff scares me. What do you think of it, Lisa?"

"The King of Chicago," she said. "What a dumb name for a leader. Why not president or premier? Is this the Dark Ages or something?"

Neither of them answered. They both knew that in many ways it was like a past time in history. And kings and brutality were again a part of life. "We'll be ready for them," she said.

"Where to now, Lisa?" Charlie asked.

"Well, we *could* look at other towns. But I really don't think we'll find anything much different than what we've seen today. We're going to have to revise our plan tonight. We'll just have to do it without a big army." Lisa thought a while.

"Driver," she said, "turn here. Left." And Lisa led the motorcade safely down streets without enemies to the farm on Swift Road.

But it wasn't the quiet farm that they had expected to find. The high flames made Lisa think of an earlier fire. The hundred voices made her think of earlier battles and past celebrations.

"Which was this?" she wondered as the motorcade came to rest in front of the farm. Was it a party or was it trouble?

It was definitely a party—that was apparent by the shouts and cheers of joy as she walked toward the crowd in the farmyard. They had been singing the Glenbard song and waiting for the return of the motorcade. The orange-and-yellow flag of Glenbard was flying high above the bonfire. Yes, they were celebrating.

Someone had learned that Lisa was safe and at a farm on Swift Road. The rumor had spread quickly through the city. "Charlie!" Lisa was angry now. "How could this happen? How did they find out? Don't you realize what could happen? It could be our *big* mistake. Logan might come here after us and, if not, he'll surely be on guard every minute against an attack. Tell me, Charlie! How could they have found out? Only you and Todd knew about it."

Charlie couldn't say anything. He stood there with his mouth open, thinking. Finally he said, "Lisa, I swear. I didn't tell a soul. I swear it. I can't imagine how they found out. I didn't even say we were going to the Arco station."

She believed him. And then she remembered Jill. "They must have tortured her," she thought.

The crowd wanted Lisa to speak to them. They cheered and shouted, "We want Lisa! We want Lisa!" But her mind was on other things—other very serious things. Would Logan come tonight? And what had happened to Jill? Was she hurt? What should they do next?

Could they still attack on May 26th? Could those hundreds in the yard serve as an army?

All through the night the crowd grew louder. They kept shouting, "Lisa! Lisa! We want Lisa!"

But she didn't speak to them. She planned and changed and replanned the new strategy. She sat alone in a room inside the farmhouse. And the words of caution came back to haunt her . . . "take no chances . . . look at all the possibilities . . . mistakes are costly . . . think . . . plan . . . be logical . . . take no chances. . . ."

Outside, the noise continued. No, she couldn't speak to them yet. When her plan was ready, she would talk. After all, you only speak when you have something to say.

Mysteriously, the crowd grew larger by the hour! How was it possible? Where did they all come from— those two hundred, and then three hundred? What had happened at the city?

The answer, if she'd had the time to look for it, could have been seen on Swift Road, across North Avenue, down the old route to Grand Avenue, and, finally, past the lake to the castle itself. That route was filled with a stream of pilgrims carrying their life's belongings—and food and guns—to find a leader who they now knew was alive. Before this, they had feared her dead. They thought she was something crazy, and strong, and very, very special.

But in the darkness of her outcast chamber, Lisa's courage wavered for a minute. "I'm not what they think," she said to herself. "I don't *know* if we can do it. I just don't *know*."

But the moment of weakness left her as she turned her thoughts to the problem—the one she *knew* she could solve. "Enough of doubting," she warned herself.

"I must make *this* plan right—perfect—no chances—no mistakes. . . ."

All that night and the next day Lisa kept to herself in the room. "Is it the 25th?" she wondered. "Tonight—by tonight I *must* have the plan ready."

The crowd of three hundred waited outside in the warm spring air. They waited patiently, never doubting that everything would be all right—that she would figure something out.

Todd came to work by her side. Together, by candlelight, they looked at plans and drawings. The conference seemed endless to those waiting outside.

"What are they doing in there?" the children asked. "Why won't she come out here? Why can't we go get that thug Logan?"

Charlie assured them: "It's an important plan. A very important plan—we can't make any mistakes—we must be very careful. We can't take any chances! You must trust her. She knows what to do."

And when Lisa was ready—when she told them the new plan—it went into effect very suddenly.

In what seemed to be almost the next moment, the crowd was at the castle. They took positions in the woods, and by the walls, and in the trees around Glenbard. There was not a single mistake . . . not a sound anywhere!

The children were outside, all around the fortress, while Lisa alone crept through the secret tunnel.

Would he be in the chamber? Was her gun loaded? Did she have the key ready? Would there be guards?

"What's wrong?" She emerged inside the fortress and was confused. "No guards anywhere! No children anywhere . . . what's the matter?" The absence of guards made her more nervous than it would have had they been everywhere.

She went through the basement section. There were no guards, no citizens. Up the stairs to the main floor—nothing, not a soul anywhere: "What's going on? . . . What's wrong? . . ." She went down the corridor. It was deserted, lifeless! Should she turn back? No!

She found her way to the old chamber and turned the key. He was sitting there as though he had been waiting. "Hello, Lisa. I've been expecting you," he said, and then he added, "sit down. I want to talk to you."

She hadn't expected this.

"I can't handle your city, Lisa. You win. Your children rebelled and just walked out. How could I stop them? What could I do?

"Lisa, I'm sorry for the shooting, truly sorry. I told them not to shoot. It was an accident . . . I didn't mean to hurt you . . . and your friend, Jill, they'll tell you that I hurt her too. But I didn't. We just scared her a little. She's safe in a room downstairs. We just scared her, Lisa, that's all . . . they were all leaving. Your citizens found out where you were—I think she told them—and I threatened to hurt her if the others left, but they were too busy running away to hear me. They just walked out. What else could I do? They hated me from the start . . . what could I do?"

"Is he asking my opinion?" she wondered. Logan seemed spent and weary. He had known the burden of the city, and he didn't care any longer. He was beaten.

"Okay, let's talk," Lisa said, and she laid the gun on the table beside the candle.

It was a trick. In a second, he grabbed the gun, aimed it at her, and shouted a signal to fifty hidden guards, who soon filled the hall outside.

And for a second time in the history of the city, the gang leader smiled victoriously at the girl.

SEVENTEEN

The door closed and Lisa and Tom were alone in the tower chamber. She forgot about the danger for a moment as she thought about hours past in front of the candle in the dark room. She had spent so many nights planning for the future and worrying and hoping.

Now she was back, but the room didn't belong to her. "Why should it?" she wondered. "How could I fall for such a simple trick?" She felt she didn't deserve the room, or the city—she had failed to *earn* them back.

"Why does it have to be this way, Tom?" she said, not knowing where the conversation would lead. "Why do we have to fight? You know I don't want to fight. Have I ever attacked you before? This time I'm only defending what's mine . . . .

"What is it about you, Tom, that makes you want to fight and steal? Are you afraid you can't earn things for yourself? Why do you need to steal what others have worked for?"

Tom listened, but he couldn't reply. She had named his weakness and that was painful.

Lisa went on. "What good is your life, Tom? Did you ever wonder about that? What fun is there in your kind of dirty business? What fun is there in making people afraid of you? Why do you need slaves, or soldiers who are afraid of you? You depend on fear!

"You start with your soldiers' fear of death and starvation . . . and then you add to that your own fear of failure and . . . I can't help but think of it, Tom . . . your fear of building your own life with your own brains.

"You know, Tom, that's what it is. You haven't the guts to depend on your own resources. No! You'd rather be tough and take what someone else has worked hard for.

"Do you have any idea what this city cost me, Tom? And I'm not talking about money either. I paid for this place with hard work. I didn't force anyone to help me—I didn't steal anything that belonged to anyone else. I used my head, Tom, and I built Glenbard.

"And then you . . . you came along with your ragged army and your guns and decided that my work was ripe for the harvest."

Tom had no answer. He put the gun down on the table.

But Lisa did not pick it up. She had a much better weapon—she understood his fear. She had Tom Logan against the wall, and she decided to drive home the final blow.

"You're afraid, Tom Logan, of life and your ability to earn your way through it. I feel sorry for you because you don't know what real fun is." And, thinking of the great king, she wanted to give him the happiness advice. But she knew he wasn't ready for it—not yet, at least.

"You're free, Tom," she said. "Go away, and take your army with you."

And as he moved to the door she said, "I'd like to be able to like you, Tom."

Within minutes, every trace of the Chidester, Elm, and Lenox army was gone from Glenbard—forever.

Lisa closed the chamber door. The gun was still on the table.

"Alone!" she said. It felt good to be back. She felt drawn to the old chair—her chair. She sat, deep in thought, while her city filled with happy citizens. The hall was crowded—they were waiting to see her.

There was a knock at the chamber door. It was Todd. "Well, we're back, aren't we, Todd?" She smiled at him.

"They want you to speak to them, Lisa."

"What? About what? They're waiting in the hall? There are hundreds out there. I must rest a minute. You should go to sleep now, Todd, over there, on the couch. I'll tell you a story tomorrow. Will that be all right?

"You must be awfully tired," she said. "You haven't slept in days, have you? I'm tired too. Maybe we can take a vacation soon. You know, I've been so very busy lately, I haven't told you what a good boy you are and. . . ."

Then Lisa noticed that he had already fallen asleep. She looked lovingly at her brave little brother.

After a time, the noise from the hall distracted her. "What do they want?" she wondered. "Can't I be alone tonight? I'm so very tired. Why must they shout like that? Why do they waste their time making a hero out of me? Why don't they spend the effort on something more constructive? How can I tell them?

"I must tell them, I know," she decided. "But, how? . . . what can I say?"

There was another knock at the door. "Come in, Eileen. What's the matter? Why are you crying? . . . Oh, that's so nice of you, Eileen. That's the nicest thing anyone's ever said to me!"

And then Lisa tried to tell the little girl what it was

that she wanted all the others to understand. "You can do most anything in the world. But you must learn the first lesson, Eileen. Never be afraid. If something bad does happen, you must ask yourself what you can do to make it into something good . . . and when something good happens, you must ask yourself what you can do to *keep* it good . . . .

"Eileen, are you listening?

". . . If the bad thing is beyond changing, then forget it—nothing can change it, not even your regret. But if the thing can be changed, then try everything in your power to make it good! You'd be surprised at what you're capable of, Eileen. Do you understand what I'm saying? . . . Are you listening? . . ."

The little girl *was* listening, but not to Lisa. She was hearing the sounds in the hall. To her it sounded like a thousand children at a party. Such a noise—what a merry mood!

"What do they want from me?" Lisa thought. "Today they follow me and cheer me, and tomorrow, they'll call me crazy . . . Just wait till they hear my new plans!

"I wish I could tell them my truth in a few, simple words, but it's impossible. Even the king's happiness advice wouldn't make sense to them. I know that. They have to discover it for themselves. They have to end the fear by themselves. They have to learn to earn for themselves. Wouldn't it be an absurd thing if I tried to *give* it to them, or if I tried to *make* them learn it? That would be the mistake the great king made. It wouldn't make sense at all. Imagine being forced into goodness or happiness!"

Eileen nestled on Lisa's lap.

"You can do it, Eileen. Anything you want to do is possible. You'll find out. Just don't be afraid. Life *is* real fun. *Reality* is fun."

Lisa wasn't sure when the little girl's dreams began. But she felt her body grow heavy in her arms, and she carried her to the couch. Todd and Eileen slept soundly together.

Lisa lit the candle. She smiled and called it her "thoughtful" candle. Its flame had inspired the plans that had shaped herself and her city.

The shouts from the hall became insistent. "We want Lisa! We want Lisa!" It sounded as though all the citizens were there, waiting and chanting.

She wanted to please them. But she didn't know what to say. Should she tell them about the "King of Chicago" and try to wake them up to the struggle that was coming?

Should she quote from her special book—the one that had put into words the truths she had sensed? "No," she decided. "That won't do it. That's not something they would understand."

She had to speak to them. It was her job. But she was so very tired—what could she say?

"Why do they keep shouting? Can't they go to bed and dream about their own plans? Why must they hear mine? Tonight, I have no plans! My life is full and I am satisfied.

"Sure, I'll talk to them. I'll give them a speech that they'll cheer and forget by the time they fall asleep. But if they're ever to know what I know, they'll have to discover some of the truth for themselves. They'll have to see me for what I am. I'm not afraid of reality. I see it. And I learn from it. And that's *real* fun!"

She paused by the door, not wanting to make her appearance—not wanting to spoil her hard-earned peace. Why couldn't they understand? It was so simple. Why was she so alone?

Lisa stood for a long time with her hand on the door

latch. She thought, "I don't know how, but I'll figure out a way to show them. I'll figure something out . . . ."

. . . . And the girl who owned the city walked through the door into the waiting crowd of children.